Loveless

Love is worth the fight ♡

[signature]

Loveless

MARISSA HOWARD

Published in the United States of America

ISBN: 978-0-9985935-0-0

Fiction / Dystopian

17.02.21

For those who choose to fight for love
instead of simply fighting.

1

I remember what it was like. The memories live in a part of my mind blacker than this world.

I was five. Before that day, I remember rivers crashing against rocks and rising from the sweat of the sand. I remember the sun sliding farther down the sky each night, stepping over clouds and the red of the air to seek a destination that is never permanent. I remember fields of wildflowers stretching their heads toward the sky and drinking in the last bit of warmth from the sun. I remember watching them each night and wondering why, with their heads turned toward the sun and their chubby stalks firmly in the ground, they were trembling. When I heard gunshots and I saw my mother crumple into the wildflowers, I never wondered again. If I knew what was coming, I would have trembled each night too.

I remember seeing them point to me, their faces twisted into grins that almost covered the perpetual scars on their cheeks and foreheads. They lit the field of wildflowers on fire. Their guns were lifted, aimed, their dirty fingers on the trigger. Then they fell back, and I didn't know why.

Hands motioned me from the field where I stood in shock. Words were whispered into my ears.

"Everything is going to be okay. Shhh. Everything is going to be okay."

The next few minutes were a blur, hands beckoning me through the town past piles of buildings crushed into the ground, flowers and trees heaped into burning mounds on the side of the road and people, screaming, with arms in front of their faces and children cowering behind them. Shrieks of laughter rang from the shadows, creating a disturbing harmony to it all.

Then I remember my breath leaving me and I came to a sudden stop in the middle of the dirt. It was the stories I had heard, forbidden by all but still told by some. I knew because of the woman grasping the damp bars of a window as the world was chaos around her.

It was her eyes.

They were a deep brown, but they were brighter than the sun. Not like ours, clouded over with fear and emptiness. They were glistening, pooled with emotion and a brokenness and sympathy that I have not been able to explain even to this day. She was looking at me with raw, compassionate, and extraordinary love. Against all odds, she had found a way to hold onto what every other person had tossed into the burning fire. She had found a way to love again.

Fear clouded her eyes and she ducked beneath the bars. The empty window looked back at me in silence.

After that, the hands took me to a place that no one remembers. No one but us.

We went down stairs for what seemed like hours. I remember thinking that if I went down any more stairs, I would drown. Not from a lack of air, but from a lack of life. When we finally reached the ground, we walked down a hallway as black as night. Lights lined the walls every few feet. They would slowly become dimmer, and just when it seemed like they were as black as the air surrounding, they would brighten again, only to blacken soon after. It was as if they were breathing.

The tunnel ended, and I saw it. A dome stretched in front of me, the gray walls and ceiling blackening like the night sky as they reached higher. Large indents were carved into the sides of the Dome. There were dozens of them, lining the walls like the brittle holes in a beehive. And inside the indents, and inside this dome, were people.

Some were sitting on the ground, eyes closed and mouth open in shock. Some were pacing, back and forth, back and forth, as if they were waiting for something. Some were simply standing, like statues rooted to the ground. Only a few looked up when I first walked into that room. Only a few of what looked like one hundred.

"This will be your home now," the hands said softly. "You're safe here. Until it's done."

Then they left me, standing alone in the silent room hundreds of feet underground with people who had managed to escape. People who were living here. People just like me.

I sat down, clutching a yellow, wilting wildflower I had grabbed before the world was destroyed.

2

I live in a world where love does not exist.

It is not even a vision, a fragment of memory, because no piece of it remains. In this world, love is a foreign object, a thing of the past that only caused pain, hopelessness, and bitter divorces ending in broken people. It was the thing that caused so many to surrender their purposes in life, because without a love they once had—the tender hand of a sweetheart to hold or a kiss to dry their dirty tears—all was lost.

So love was destroyed. Taken away as quickly as people feel it.

But what we did not know is that the world would be destroyed along with it. Without love, the good, the beauty in this life suddenly seemed ugly. And everything that was dirty, destructive, and lifeless suddenly seemed beautiful.

It was an inverse of life that sucked the very breath from the living.

Trees were uprooted, flowers burned in fires along the roadside, and the sky filled with black smoke until it was no longer a mint blue but the color of dirt.

And the people—that was the biggest destruction of them all. You could see it in their eyes. What had once been pools of hope and specks of delight became distant, darkened with each night that passed and stripped of feeling with each day.

They couldn't laugh anymore. They couldn't pick a child up and throw him in the sky because they saw no reason to. They couldn't grasp the fingers of another because it was disgusting. Repulsive. To feel the warmth of another was like touching fire, and they didn't want to get burnt.

So they destroyed the world, and they took each other with it, until no one was left.

No one but us.

This is what they tell us every morning, so we don't forget. But what do they know? We haven't been above ground—haven't touched the light of day, haven't seen the black sky or the piles of destruction or heard the endless screams—in thirteen years.

3

I woke with a bitter chill running down my spine.

The blankets were wrapped around me and soaked in sweat, clinging to my shaking skin. I sat up and threw them off me. They landed in a heap on top of the empty bed mounted on the wall next to mine. The bed where my mother would have slept. But she was killed thirteen years ago. I shook the memory of her, light brown hair caught by the wind as she collapsed into the bright yellow flowers, from my mind.

I pulled on charcoal-colored pants and a matching shirt, snapped my hair in a bun, and flicked the switch that opened the door to my indent in the Dome. There were no mirrors here. There hadn't been mirrors since I was taken here when I was five.

No one said hello to each other as we walked to breakfast simultaneously. It was like this every day. Wake up, get dressed, walk to breakfast, eat, go to studies, walk to dinner, go to the center of the Dome for Collaboration, go to bed. Everyone wore the same gray pants and long-sleeved shirt, and no one said to each other more than they had to. Apart from answering questions in class, the halls were silent. They had always been silent, because that is the only peace we knew.

We were told it wasn't always this way. There had once been a time when people enjoyed talking to each other and understanding a past life that one had once lived, a past that somehow defined and enhanced their future. People would embrace one another when they saw sadness or touch a hand when they wanted to show concern. When they wanted to show love. But love does not exist. It hasn't existed since we as a people voted to cut it out of life altogether, seventy-four years ago.

It's amazing how easy it was to do. When people don't have relationships to cry about or family members to mourn over, life is simple. But each day that passed hearts grew cold and faces grew lifeless. Violence enveloped the purpose of many of the people that lived. Life was so simple that many started to believe that all of the good—all of the things that once represented love—in this world should be destroyed. Thirteen years ago was the peak of the destruction. The beginning of the end of the world.

The faces were unmoving as we walked to the food line and grabbed a plate, a gray napkin, and some silverware. We had heard stories of the past about smiles and laughter, about tears of joy, about a heart beating frantically out of pure delight. But none of us had ever experienced any of it. It was as foreign to us as the world above ground now was.

"Laney." The person chosen to serve food today nodded as she checked off my name from the list of the ninety-seven people that lived in this dome. We started with one hundred, but thirteen years is a long time. I didn't even know the names of the people who died. We assumed that old age took them—dying from anything else down here just seemed impossible.

I chose the seat next to the door, by an older woman with graying hair and hands that looked like they had been through more than what we accomplished here each day. Much more. I wondered for a brief moment what her life was like before she was taken down here. I had been only five. She was old enough to have lived when peace did exist. When love existed. But it didn't matter anymore. I let the thought slip away before it even touched the surface of my mind.

A bell rang through the dining hall and we all stood. It was time to go to studies. The halls crowded with silent people once again. Everyone went, with different age groups in different rooms.

There were six in my room. We didn't know what the other groups of people learned because we never talked to them. We just knew that we needed to keep our minds sharp. If we didn't, we might become like the people that had emptied their minds of everything but disorder and force; we might become like the people that had scraped the world and left nothing in its place. And if we did, there would be no one left. The world would be done, humanity a whisper that weaved through the piles of ashes above ground. We were what was left, and we held onto this truth above all else.

Our teacher was one of twelve people in the Dome that had actually been a teacher in his past life. He had managed to save books and manuscripts, along with the other eleven. Books written solely for reading enjoyment were not part of the collection, as those kinds of books were burned in a fire when they made the vote to end love. Most of those books, I had heard, were about love and relationships and therefore contradicted the law.

There were no history books either. That was our biggest mistake, coming down here without a trace of humanity's history in factual form. We learned math and English, typical subjects that were once taught to kids above ground. At least that's what I was told. I was supposed to start school a few months after the world turned upside down.

"Dalia. Gavin. Laney. Nash. Theodore. Alese."

Our teacher checked us off the list as each of us walked through the door and took a seat in our given spots. He was a tall man, probably in his forties, with a beard the color of the dark ceiling in the Dome. The only things we knew about him were that he was a teacher before he came to live down here, and his name: Mr. Dabir. He had insisted over the past thirteen years that people who had once lived in a peaceful world called each other by names, and the idea was agreed on by everyone in the Dome. Now, every time someone entered a room or came to the front of a line, you would simply say their name, nothing else.

This was how much of our world underground worked. The ninety-seven people who lived in this dome had one major thing in common: they all wanted peace. They all wanted life to go back to the way it had been more than seventy-four years ago, when love was as real as the person next to them and yet somehow, the world was peaceful.

But what is love? None of us had lived in a time when this mystery word existed. We only had stories, memories that were carried from generation to generation, banned by all but still told by some. It was like putting something together with only a few of the pieces. So we tried to remember. This was the purpose of Collaboration, held each night before we went to our indents to sleep. To scrape up memories of a life that none of us had ever lived—a world that none of us had ever seen. To remember how to love again. Because as far as we knew, humanity needed love to survive.

Our people would share stories their grandmother had told or simply come up with an idea that they believed in. Then everyone would vote. All ninety-seven people had to agree for a vote to be cast into law. Any disagreement would cause disruption, and that was far from peace. And anything far from peace was, as far as we knew, far from love.

"They all walked together, as much as they could, so no one ever fell behind," one bald, round-faced man had said one night at Collaboration.

The vote was taken, and everyone agreed.

"They wore the same outfits so no one could outdo another," a short redhead in her thirties had said another night.

It only seemed natural. Why allow one to be more beautiful than another, only to cause jealousy, which contrasted peace? Later that night, I had watched my cotton white skirt, yellow shirt, scuffed-up black shoes, and bright blue bow that had once been tangled in my long brown hair be burned in the furnace room, the room that was farthest from the Dome's center.

This was how our lives underground had gone since we first came down here. They were shaped and molded by Collaboration each night, or more simply, by people who believed they knew the secret to how humanity once survived in a world with love. This was also how, seventy-four years ago, love had been voted out of existence. In the past we had always governed ourselves, had always held Collaborations where everyone was present. It was all we knew, so we carried on this form of governing down here. And so far, it seemed to be working. Thirteen years and not a single sign of anyone falling down the path of destruction and disharmony.

I took a seat at my desk and listened. Anything to write on or with was banned by all of us years ago. Allowing someone to write caused them to get ideas, and ideas meant differences of opinion, which could lead to disagreements. Simply taking in knowledge, a gray-haired man with trembling hands had said at Collaboration one night, should be enough.

Mr. Dabir looked at all of us with the same facial expression we saw each and every day for the past thirteen years. But this time was different. This time, his eyes seemed to linger on each of us a little bit longer. He blinked, cleared his throat like he had always done. Then he spoke. And what he said was different from anything I had ever learned in my time in the Dome; different from anything we had ever voted on or discovered or made into existence. What he said ripped my life out from under me and made me feel hopelessly and dismally lost.

"Give all of the subject books in your desk to me," he said, his voice unchanging. "You will not be needing them today."

4

The room grew even more silent than it normally was.

But then, slowly, the other people in the classroom began opening their desks, setting their books with a thud on the top of the chalky gray surface, one by one, and then lifting them in their arms to take to the front of the room.

We were taught that obedience, above many things, kept the peace, so it seemed only natural. Dalia, a tall girl with blond hair in a tight bun who sat in front of me, looked at her books for a moment too long before she carried them up with everyone else. I was the last to arrive. I sat my math book and the book that taught us proper grammar and spelling on our teacher's desk. I suddenly felt lost, as if I had just let go of one of the few pieces that made up my life.

Mr. Dabir watched us all with a blank expression in his eyes and looked at the books that were piled up on his desk. His eyes lingered, but he tore them away.

"We have reason to believe that the war above ground is over," he said, his voice steady. "Our supplies are getting low, and there is no life for us down here anymore."

I swallowed. I knew there was only so much time until the food and water would run dry. I had never imagined that it actually would. Mr. Dabir paused, his eyes searching every one of us.

"We need to see if what we think we know is true—that everyone is dead. They couldn't have survived more than a few years. They should be long gone by now." He ran his fingers along the desk. "But many of the people down here…" He stopped. His hands went to his hair. "Are terrified. They don't remember a life without murder, without destruction. More than just making sure the world is safe now, our people need to be convinced. They need to want to go above ground. To believe in it. Otherwise our community will fall, and humans will cease to exist."

Mr. Dabir paused again.

"But that's not all." His eyes ran along the cracking, gray walls and stopped on me. "Even if the above ground is safe, we now know that humanity needs love to survive. And love does not exist down here. No matter how hard we try and find it."

It looked as though he was trying to feel the next words that passed over his tongue—to taste them, to make sure they were real.

"We are going to send six people above ground to do two things." Mr. Dabir held up his fingers slowly. Locked the eyes of the person next to me. "Make sure the world is safe again. And find love. Or whatever's left of it after seventy-four years."

Silence filled the air, more than the normal silence that surrounded us each and every day. I didn't turn my head. Didn't look at the person next to me. My eyes were on Mr. Dabir. His chest, breathing in and out slightly faster than it usually did. And his face, as calm as the stack of books at his back. Then he turned in one swift motion and his hand pointed toward the door.

"We will go immediately to Collaboration to vote on the six that will perform these two tasks. A person will only be chosen if they demonstrate something about the humanity that existed when love existed." His thick eyebrows creased. "The people that go on this journey—we need to be sure they will not turn for the worse while they are up there." His eyebrows smoothed again. He looked up. "Whoever does this best, well, best of luck to you as you enter once again the world we left thirteen years ago."

Dalia's hand was on her lips. Theodore, a short boy with red hair sitting next to me, shifted uncomfortably in his chair.

I sat, unmoving. Even if we wanted to go above ground, none of us had been alive before hatred took over the world. The only history we had of this time were stories, word of mouth that we had heard from people like our grandmother. If these others had even had a chance to talk to their grandmother before she was killed. There was no telling what was up there now. No telling what awaited the six. I swallowed.

There was no telling what love was, or where it was. Or if it even still was.

Slowly the classroom emptied as each person stood up and began walking toward the center of the Dome where Collaboration was held each night. I was one of the last to leave, and I headed for the door.

"Laney."

I stopped abruptly, shocked. It was the first time someone had said my name at a time other than roll call in more than ten years. And no one was in front of me now.

I turned around sharply. Nash. Sandy blond hair and brown eyes, a few inches taller than me with his gray shirt tucked loosely in his pants. He had been in my class since we came down here. He looked a year or two older than me, but that was fitting for our age group. Classes stayed together, with the same teacher, for the entire thirteen years. It was that way so there would be no confusion or distraction switching teachers every few years. I had never talked to Nash before. I had never talked to any of them. I had heard about "friends" in the past, but none of us understood it. Why would someone want to cause jealousy by talking to one person but not to another? We had voted against it during the very first week. I just looked at him.

"It is Laney, right?" He had heard my name every day in class, but it seemed foreign hearing it now. I nodded.

"Do you want to...go above ground?" He was looking into my eyes, but since it had been so long since conversation, it was difficult for both of us. My throat was dry. My mouth did not open. I didn't know what I wanted; it was still hard to understand what I had just heard. But then an image came into my mind. An image I had not seen in a very long time.

It was my mother, just months before the men killed her as they were passing through. She was wearing a light blue dress with a yellow bow that tied in the back. It was just my mother and I. I never had a father. Since there was no love, fathers helped populate the earth and then left—the only form of touch that was not forbidden, but only once in every lifetime. The mothers raised the children until they were old enough to go out on their own.

She was taking a picture of us for the mantle, like every mother had voted to do in case an accident happened inside the house and someone needed to take count of who lived there. My mother had set the camera up on a rock facing the wildflowers. Just as she was running to get into place next to me before the flash went off, a flock of birds burst out of the flowers behind us. She shrieked, her hands over her head as she dove to the ground. I was terrified. We both crouched there for a few seconds, catching our breath. Then my mother calmly stood up, smoothed out her dress, and walked over to the camera. She pressed a few buttons and then walked over to me, holding the camera out for me to see. The picture showed her and me, arms flailing and hair flying in the wind, with birds just a few feet above us in open flight. My mother's mouth was parted in a scream, her eyes wide like the sun. Then she looked at me and winked.

I didn't know what that wink meant. I still don't. I had never even seen someone wink before. But I couldn't help but try to believe that it had something to do with love. And in that moment, for the first time in years, I tried to believe it again.

I forced my eyes up to Nash's and nodded. My mother had held onto something—some sort of love or form of life that I had never seen again—and I needed to find it.

"Okay," he breathed, unsure of exactly what he wanted to say next. "I think I know how to get everyone to vote for us. I think I know how to be best at the task. But I can't do it alone. I need you to come up there with me."

Alone was all we knew. "With me" were words I had seen in our writing book, but we had never used these words down here, no more than to describe how we all walked to places side by side. I was confused and my breathing was faster than normal, like Mr. Dabir's had been. But I nodded again before I gave myself a chance to think.

5

Almost everyone had gathered in the center of the Dome already, a place with only enough seats for each person and a large, handmade platform out of something dull and gray in the middle of the circle of chairs. I took a seat next to Nash, and we all waited in silence.

After a few moments passed, one of the other teachers, Ms. Geena, a short woman with choppy brown hair and a pudgy chin, walked to the platform. She cleared her throat.

"Let us begin."

Three words, and she lifted a clipboard from the podium and began reading names one by one. It was the clipboard that kept track of each person who lived down here. The one they used at meals to check us off each day.

"Ethel. Anna. Beatrice. Kalee."

Each name she read was a chance for that person to get up and prove that he or she knew more about a peaceful humanity, about love, than anyone else. She paused between each one. Ten more names passed, and no one had moved. It was like she was calling roll call to an empty classroom. Mr. Dabir was right—they were terrified of the world above.

"Nadia. Felicity. Gavin." There was movement in the crowd. Gavin stood up and began to walk toward the platform. Gavin from my classroom. He looked about as tall as me, with dark brown hair and milky white skin. He looked back at the crowd once while he

walked, and his eyes were brooding. I had never seen them before—
he had always faced the front of the room.

When Gavin reached the podium, he stepped onto it with
distrust. He smoothed his hair slowly and looked out at all of us.

"I don't know much about the time when love existed, or
whatever, but I'm strong," his eyes never faltered, never looked
down. "And I know that humanity, ever since the beginning of
time, has survived in some part because the people were strong.
Weak people don't survive. As we saw thirteen years ago."

He nodded his head once, as a courtesy, and then left the
platform. The audience was quiet. They had nothing to say, and
neither did I.

Ms. Geena began saying names again after a few seconds. An
older man I had seen and knew nothing about went up to the
platform when his name was called and told a story his grandmother
had told him about people picking flowers for a reason other than
to throw them in the fire. Perhaps, he said, people had thought they
were good to look at, and not nuisances. He was stumped, however,
when he realized he could not explain why good people would want
to pick a flower when it would only kill the flower faster.

Mallory, a redhead from the age group right above us, was the
first woman to take the platform. She simply held out her hands in
silence. Then a few moments passed, and she spoke. She told of a
time when her hands were smooth and soft, but were now riddled
with bumps and calluses on the surface.

"I cleaned, every night like we had voted on," she said, speaking
of the time before the world was destroyed. "I was nine. I scrubbed
dishes until my hands hurt, and I never asked anyone to take my
place. I imagine humanity before destruction was much like that.
You can't trust people to get things done. You have to do it yourself."

When she finished talking, she wiped her hands on her gray
pants as if that would make the calluses disappear.

Only twelve more people stood up when their names were called,
twelve of ninety-seven. Twelve more people who tried to think of
something that embodied the humans before us better than the one

before. Dalia, the girl from my class, demonstrated what she called "clapping," when people would slap their hands together in a way that meant someone did a good job. She had seen her grandmother do it to her once, when Dalia had learned the difference between herbs that everyone grew outside of their houses, to "be as self-sustaining as possible," it was explained when they had voted for it. The moment her grandmother brought her hands together, her mother had slapped them. That was all she remembered, but she knew it was something from the times before. Why else would her mother have grown angry?

An older man stood on the platform and said he once had a wagon, but he didn't remember why.

Theodore, the short redhead from my class, even stood up. He walked to the front of the room with his head down, and he didn't look back. When he got to the edge of the podium, he didn't step up on it. He didn't say a word. He just stood there for a few moments, his eyes on the gray, stone ground that matched the Dome's cold walls.

And then he lifted his chin, and something happened. Something came from his mouth that was not a word, spoken like we all knew how to speak. It was higher in pitch, haunting in tone. It seemed to reach toward the ceiling and then stretch along the walls, run down them, like a paint no one could see. He was talking, but not talking. I had never heard such a thing. A chill swept up my arms and then it was gone. He stopped. The air around us grew eerily silent. Theodore never looked up, but he spoke, for one brief moment.

"My mother did that to me once. There were people walking by outside, and they came in the house and killed her. I don't know what it was," his mouth trembled, then stilled. "But it was forbidden. It was not from our time."

He stood beside the platform for a moment longer, then walked back to his seat and sat down, his head still facing the ground.

Ms. Geena did not start speaking again until minutes after that happened. I looked down and realized I was clutching the side of the seat. I quickly took my hand off and placed it in my lap again.

I was still thinking about what Theodore had done when Nash's name was called. He stood up quickly, like he was waiting for this moment. Then he looked back at me once, reminding me of our agreement. I hesitated. Doubt flooded my mind, but I stood up.

Ms. Geena looked confused and opened her mouth to say something, but stopped. Her eyes were on the audience, and she nodded slowly then backed away. It was if someone had told her to let it happen. To let us go up there side by side, even though my name had not been called. We stepped onto the platform and Nash stopped. He nodded when I stopped next to him and faced the people. I straightened my shirt.

Nothing happened. Nash did nothing. Minutes passed, and we stood there side by side, everyone looking on in silence. I was about to turn to Nash, to see if I was missing something, when he moved. He lifted his arm up in the air slowly, carefully, like it was made of glass. He was making sure everyone was watching it. He stood there with his arm raised for a minute. And then he swept his arm down quickly, instantaneously, and grabbed my hand.

Heat washed through my arm and up to my brain, static shook my insides in such strength that I thought I might pass out. He raised our hands together so they were pointing toward the roof of the Dome. Toward the sky.

He held our arms there together for a few seconds, and then it all caught up to me. I gasped and pulled my arm from his, the heat still reverberating through my body. I had not been touched since I was born. Even then, they had used gloves. Mothers never held children, they were in cribs. Touching someone else was forbidden, voted out of humanity seventy-four years ago and voted out by us thirteen years ago. It was the very foundation of jealousy and destruction. And now, after seventy-four years, it had happened again. It had happened to me.

Gasps rang through the audience and a few people stood. I walked quickly to my seat and sat down without looking up. My hand was tingling. Burning. A fire had just been lit, and I had been standing in the middle of it.

6

Ms. Geena looked as terrified as the rest of them. Of course, fear was one of the only things we knew—one of the only things we had always been able to feel. Fear of the unknown and fear of what we did know. Fear, and anger.

"Will everyone please take a seat. Remember—silence is the way to peace. As we all agreed."

She seemed to be striving to grasp onto some sort of reason or sense of normalcy. She looked at the other teachers, quickly regained her composure and nodded.

"We will take the vote."

I was still in shock. A state of disbelief. My hand was limp at my side. They were going to ignore it? It felt like my life had been turned upside down. I had not felt my heart beat like that since thirteen years ago, when the guns pierced the gray sky. I was terrified with the rest.

One by one, names were called and each person walked to the platform in the center of us all, wrote down a single name, and went back to their seats.

Thirteen years has an impact on a person like no one could ever explain. One moment was chaos, people standing on their feet and wondering if what they had just seen was real. It was a jolt of electricity, a gust of wind that slammed into trees on an otherwise calm day. And then the electricity stilled, the gust passed, and all was normal again. All was as it had been, and as it should be.

Nash sat beside me, his face unchanging. But when I looked down, his hand shook. It was for just a second, and anyone else would have missed it. If he had lived by the law, he had not been touched but once in his life either. I was angry for the first time in years, and yet I wondered if it had been as hard for him as it had been for me.

"Laney." Ms. Geena spoke my name and looked up, looked me in the eye. I stood up slowly, carefully, and walked to the platform. I could feel all eyes on me.

Ms. Geena held the pen hesitantly, as if she had second thoughts about letting me vote. But then she placed it in my hand. A statement would only become a law if everyone voted, all ninety-seven of us. She knew that as well as anyone else.

I looked down at the white paper, my hand still trembling. Remembering who else had taken a chance on the podium was almost impossible after what had happened. But then an image struck my mind—an image of a boy with red hair, his mouth open and his green eyes on the ground. Theodore. I scribbled his name on the paper and walked back to my seat. After what Nash did, I wasn't sure if I even wanted to go above ground anymore. We couldn't vote for ourselves, anyway. We had voted against it seventy-four years ago and kept the same law when we came down here. Being conceited was a trait that did not agree with peace.

Nash put in his vote shortly after me, followed by Dalia and Theodore and the rest of the people. Last to write down her vote was a girl from my class with long brown hair pulled into a bun and soft brown eyes. Alese. She was one of the fifteen who had gone up to the platform when her name was called. Quietly, she had talked about a memory she had when she was four.

She and her mother had gone to town to buy milk and material to make blankets. They were on a dusty path, three miles from town, when it had started to rain. The rain turned into deep, murky puddles and their vehicle became stuck. Then a man had driven by. Men and women did not talk to each other; it was voted against and forbidden. And this man did not break that law. But when he drove by, he had stopped. He reached out his window and placed a brown bag of warm pastries on her mother's lap. He drove off without a word, and they never saw him again. Alese had said this was her most vivid memory of her life before the Dome. Though she didn't know what it meant, she knew that she had never experienced anything like it since.

When she walked back from writing her vote on the paper, her eyes were on Nash and me. She didn't look away until she sat down, her back to us.

Ms. Geena gathered the papers and straightened them on the podium.

"The other eleven teachers and I will determine the votes and announce them at a Collaboration we will hold tomorrow morning after breakfast. The six names that occur most often in the votes will then prepare to go above ground immediately afterward." She took a breath. "You are dismissed to your indents."

I wanted to get out of the room as quickly as I could, to get away from Nash. From the guy who had caused me to break a law that had been in place for almost a century.

I walked to the door and spilled out into the hallway with everyone else. Silence filled the room once again, but the sounds of footprints bounced off the stone walls.

Suddenly Mr. Dabir was by my side. He simply said my name once then motioned to a classroom on the right. I shut my eyes briefly, then opened them and followed. I had never been pulled away from the hallway before, in all thirteen years. We were all supposed to walk together, as the bald man had said. This was almost more than I could take.

I walked through the door and saw Nash standing by the empty desks, as gray as the area surrounding. My fists tightened and I forced my eyes to Mr. Dabir. He looked at both of us, back and forth, then stopped.

"I don't know what that was back there, but the other teachers and I agree that it wasn't good. Touch does not embody peace. In any way, shape, or form," he paused and breathed deeply. "You will both vote, with each other, to never do it again. And then we will continue life as it was, and as it should be."

I stood, paralyzed. Silence. Nash spoke first.

"Mr. Dabir," he rung his hands together once then locked eyes with our teacher. "If I may. You said our task was to demonstrate something about the humanity that existed when love existed. That was what I did."

Mr. Dabir's face reddened, but he stayed calm. "Touch is not a piece of love. It is the very foundation of a path to jealousy and destruction. People touched to kill. They touched to seduce. To force something upon someone that was unwanted. We have no history of touch as a good thing. Or do you know something that I do not know?"

Nash opened his mouth and then closed it. He put his hands in his pockets.

"No."

Mr. Dabir breathed again. "Good." He looked at me and nodded, waiting.

"I vote, once again, to ban touch." I said quietly, my head down. Nash repeated what I said. I could feel Mr. Dabir's eyes on our backs as we walked out of the room and back into the hallway.

I didn't sleep that night. My hand felt raw, changed, like it would never be the same.

7

The morning came quickly. No one knew when it was daytime or when the night sky covered the earth, so the bell was our form of time. The bell rang once to wake us up, to go from breakfast to studies, from studies to dinner, and from dinner to Collaboration. As long as the bell rang, we were on track, on time, and in sync with the sun and moon above. As long as the bell rang, all was as it should be.

We all went to breakfast, checked in, and took our plates. We all sat down and ate without looking up. But this time, some people seemed to eat more quickly than others. The people down here had never before had something to look forward to.

The bell sounded and echoed around the room before fading into silence. We walked down the hallway to the center of the Dome, took a seat, and waited. By now, waiting was something we were very good at.

This time, Mr. Dabir stepped up to the podium. It must have been his turn to lead Collaboration today. He held the same clipboard in his hands, looked at all of us.

"If the six names that I call will come up and stand next to me after I say each name." He spoke like he was calling names to help with a demonstration in class, not to go above ground after thirteen years. But then again, I had never seen him flustered. Not before yesterday.

Mr. Dabir cleared his throat and read the first name on the list.

"Gavin."

The boy from my class stood and walked to the front of the room. There was no surprise on his face; his eyes, facing forward, were unreadable. He looked determined, eager. Too much like the men had looked when they murdered my mother. I looked away when his eyes met mine. If what Gavin had said was true, at least the six going above ground would have some form of protection.

"Mallory." The woman who had talked about doing what she was told, doing what was voted upon. The fact that the majority of the people down here had chosen obedience as a means of peace was not a surprise. She took her place next to Gavin.

"Dalia." People must have liked the idea of getting praised for doing something well. Dalia stood, smoothed her shirt, and walked to the front. Her steps were light, airy. Three more.

"Alese." Alese sat in her chair for a moment, maybe in disbelief. No one here could fathom what it was like to stop their life, even for a moment, to make someone else's life better. Even Alese probably couldn't. And yet they had voted for her. They had voted for a life where that may not have been acceptable, but where it was done anyway.

"Arsen." A male from Mallory's age group who had gone up to the platform and simply stood there, in silence, before returning to his seat. Silence was one thing we all knew and loved. Of course they had chosen Arsen.

Mr. Dabir paused before reading the last name on the list. My eyes fell. There was only one name left. That meant Nash was not voted in, and so neither was I.

"Theodore." The small boy from my age group walked timidly to the center and stood next to the other five. His eyes never left the ground. He was the only one whose choosing I could not explain. But I had voted for him, hadn't I?

Mr. Dabir looked at the six who stood next to him; the six who would soon see what none of us had seen in thirteen years. The six who would go above ground to ensure peace, and maybe, to find what remained of love. He stretched his arm out, gesturing to them.

"These are the men and women you have chosen. The men and women who will discover a world that is safe, a world that has potential for peace, and a world where love might be found. They will leave in three days, the time beforehand spent preparing for what they might expect. Then they will return." Mr. Dabir paused, the people taking in each and every word. "The six will be gone for weeks, at the most. No more and no less than it takes."

Mr. Dabir dismissed us and the six stood next to him, unmoving. People began standing and leaving the room in the same way we had come. Half of the audience was in the hallway when the bell sounded. I stopped, confused. The bell was not supposed to ring when Collaboration ended. Dismissal was always enough.

People in the hallway began turning, and it was the first time in thirteen years that our hallway was in disarray. People had never gone different directions in the hallway; we all went to the same places at the same time. For the first time since we came down here, we didn't know where to go.

After standing for a few moments in uncertainty, we filed back into the center of the Dome. Maybe there we would be told where to go, what to do. Mr. Dabir still stood at the center with the six, his hands clutching the clipboard tightly. He suddenly seemed uneasy, apprehensive.

We all sat, waiting. He looked up, his eyes rounder than they usually were.

"There are two more names on this list," he said, speaking too slowly. "We will allow eight to go above ground, instead of six." Mr. Dabir stopped, looked out, someone nodded in the crowd. It did not look like these were words the teacher wanted to say. His eyes passed over the crowd and stopped on me.

"Laney and Nash. Will you come up and join us?"

8

No one breathed. No one moved. For the first time in thirteen years, the faces in the other chairs turned to look at me. They stared, eyes unmoving. And for the first time in thirteen years, I was able to see the faces of the people I lived with for more than just a brief second, as passing someone in the cafeteria would get you.

Their faces were of similar color to the gray clothes we all wore each day, lightened only by the cool air that seemed to soak through the stone walls inside the Dome. The men all had short hair, cut close to their heads. The women had hair of typical colors, red, brown, blond, and gray, but each strand was pulled back into a firm bun.

It was their eyes that stood out to me, though. Their eyes were cold, unmoving. They seemed duller than they should be. But not dull enough to want to consume themselves with violence. It was like each person here had hit a point, between top and bottom, full of life and lifeless, and just stayed there. This, our lives, were on the pathway back to peace, we had been told again and again. And voted for it too. But was this peace? I could not help but wonder if my face, my eyes, looked as terrifying as the rest.

I sat there for a moment, staring back at the faces, but Mr. Dabir motioned hastily, like he wanted to get it over with. I walked slowly, but not slowly enough. What had happened? We had just been warned against doing what we had done yesterday. This wasn't Mr. Dabir's idea. I knew that for certain.

Nash was sitting two rows ahead of mine, so he reached the platform first. He stopped next to the rest and turned, his face unreadable as it always was. When I reached the line, I stood on his right side, at the end of the row.

Mr. Dabir seemed tired. He swept his hand up, more quickly this time, and then brought it down to the clipboard once again.

"Your chosen eight."

Even the other six were looking at us now.

The next few days were a blur. We were on a different schedule than everyone else now because we suddenly had something to work toward other than studies and meals. The eight of us walked together in the hallway, apart from the other eighty-nine people. We ate our meals at a separate table from the rest. We exercised after each meal in a room next to the classrooms that was designated for keeping healthy. At Collaboration each night, we were asked to stay behind. Whichever teacher was designated to speak that night would say the same sentence, just once, and then dismiss us to our indents:

"Time is running short. Make sure you are ready."

They gave us three days to prepare for a journey above ground that could take weeks. Three days to prepare for a world that we knew nothing about anymore.

The last day came quickly. The eight of us were at our last exercise session, some running, some lifting weights, some riding stationary bikes. We were together each day, but no one talked to one another. We had been told, on the night we were chosen, that we could say to each other only what was absolutely necessary. But after not saying more than we had to for years and the idea of a world unknown at the forefront of our minds in everything we did, no one had anything to say. Nothing had changed in that sense.

I was riding one of the stationary bikes, moving my legs back and forth on the pedals while the machine buzzed beneath me. The room was no larger than one of the classrooms, so the breathing of the other seven was heard in short bursts throughout the room. I was changing the setting on my bike to one that was more difficult when someone broke the silence. At first, I wondered if I was hearing something. A machine, maybe, that had malfunctioned for a moment. But it hadn't. Someone had spoken.

"Do you feel like you're ready?"

It was Nash. Of course it was. Where he had gotten the idea, the courage, to talk much more than was needed was beyond me, especially since we had not been voted into the original six.

The rest of the room stilled, everyone looking at Nash. For a moment, I thought no one was going to answer him. I almost started pedaling again, ready to shrug off his question, when Arsen responded.

"I was born ready." He looked down at the weight he was holding then pulled it to his chest one more time. "Honestly though," he looked at Nash, then back at the weight. "I don't think saying how ready we are is what they would call 'necessary talk.' We're going, ready or not."

Arsen grabbed another weight and continued lifting, his eyes looking ahead like nothing had happened. The room slowly whirred back into motion. I glanced over at Nash and he turned his running machine back on again, started jogging.

Then another voice joined the ringing of the machines. This time it was Theodore.

"Do any of you..." He paused, searching for the words, but maybe also because speaking to others in the same room had not been normal for the majority of our lives. Other than when some had spoken at Collaboration that one night. But even then, it wasn't a conversation. Many people down here, I had thought, had simply forgotten how to have one.

"Do any of you...," Theodore continued, speaking no more softly than he had before, "remember? Like really remember? What was up there?"

Three questions. But three more questions than any of us had answered during our time in the Dome from anyone but our teachers.

The others in the room kept running, kept lifting, kept stretching. Theodore, whose eyes had lifted for just a moment when he had asked the question, brought them down again.

"Never mind."

I wondered what had brought him to ask that question—to ask about the world before. Aside from determining the ways of peace every night at Collaboration, we never talked about it. And not just because we never talked. Anything that had to do with the world before that did not have to do with peace was irrelevant, pointless. To talk about the destruction of the world—the murders, the screaming, and the burned piles of anything and everything—would only bring anger to our own lives. And anger would turn us into them.

Alese turned to Theodore from her position on the ground, stretching. Her brown eyes were soft—softer than most of the other eyes down here that I had seen.

"Do you know what a tree is?" She looked up to the ceiling like she was trying to remember, trying to form some sort of image in her mind.

Theodore was a few years younger than us, so he would have only been two or three before he was brought down here. He must not remember much.

"A month before I was brought here, my mother took me on a walk. Everything around our house—the herbs, the grass, everything—had been burned by then." Alese spoke simply, quietly.

I swallowed. Our field, the one with the yellow wildflowers, was one of the last to be burned. Somehow, we had stayed out of reach longer than the others.

"We lived by a forest," Alese continued. "It was all burned to ashes by the time I was three years old. But that day, we walked farther than we had ever walked before. We came across what once had been water, I think. There was a dry, sandy area with rocks. But next to the sand, at the edge of the rocks and in the middle of the ashes, was a tree." She stopped, narrowed her eyes, looked more deeply into the ceiling, into nothing.

"At least that's what my mother called it. I didn't know what it was, had never seen one before. Or if I had, I didn't remember. This tree—it was alive. It had long arms that stretched to the sky and green things at the end of each arm, small things shaped like hearts."

Leaves. She didn't know what they were called. By this time everyone was looking at Alese, listening. I knew what a tree was because we were the last to be attacked, but most of the others here had probably never heard of such a thing. People had started burning all forms of nature before any of us were born. The question was how long the hatred and violence took to spread to your town. For some, it was weeks. For others, mere days. From what we understood, we were brought down here when the violence in each of our towns became dangerous, lethal. Some had been down here longer than others. I had been the very last one.

Alese looked down at Theodore, her eyes back out of the world they had dropped into for a moment.

"This tree, standing in the middle of the black ground, looked like it was lost. I wonder if it realized that out of all the trees in the world, it had survived." She paused, her eyes brightening for a moment, only to dim again quickly after. "It learned to grow in a pile of ashes."

The room had ceased to a halt by now. Arsen had set down his weights. Nash was standing, frozen, on the running machine. Dalia was reaching for a button on the bike next to mine, her hand poised in the air. Gavin and Mallory were looking at Alese.

Theodore was standing by the wall, staring, and I wondered for a brief moment what he had been doing. Why he hadn't been exercising with the rest of us.

The bell rang, its high sound circling the walls and soaking up every last voice, every word. Mr. Dabir entered the room and the heavy gray door swung shut behind him. He looked at all of us, hesitated for a second because we weren't moving, exercising like we should have been. But then he found his voice.

"There will be no Collaboration tonight, as sleep is of the utmost importance. You are dismissed to your indents." He started to turn the doorknob but stopped, looked back once more.

"Tomorrow morning, immediately after breakfast, you will go above ground. You are ready."

The door echoed behind him as he left, his footsteps pounding the cold floor. I looked at Theodore. His eyes had not left Alese. To him, looking at her was looking at a whole new world.

9

That night, I woke to what sounded like screaming.

It had been so long since I had heard something like it that I lay still, wondering if it had just been a dream. But then the air was pierced with agony and suffering once again. After hearing mostly silence throughout my life, I was terrified. Disturbed. A chill swept through my skull, down my back, and out my hands. Out the hand that had been touched. I sat up in my bed. There it was again. Louder this time, like it was coming from down the hall. I couldn't take it anymore. I needed the screaming to stop. It flooded my mind with too many memories, memories that didn't need to resurface tonight.

I stood and pulled my clothes over the gray-colored nightgown we had been given to sleep in. These were the only two sets of clothing that we had, but for us down here with no intent to impress, it was enough.

The sliding doors to each of our indents locked only from the inside, so we could leave whenever we wanted. We had all voted on that when we came down here. There was no reason for us to be locked up; nothing to hide. We were all equal, every one of us. The form of order that we had, aside from Collaboration, was respect. We had voted to respect those with more knowledge than yourself, which, for all of us, meant the twelve teachers. Still, we all respected one another. Because of the studies, we were all knowledgeable in some way.

I pressed the button on the side of the wall and the door slid open. I stood for a moment, watching. Listening. Then I stepped into the hallway a few feet from my indent before anyone could see me. We were free to leave whenever, but no one ever did. The door slid to a close behind me. Silence. I had never been out of my indent at night. The hallways looked just as they did during the day—the same dim, yellow bulbs pulsing slowly as if they were breathing, the same cold, smooth stone walls. I started to turn back. This was a mistake.

The yell plummeted through the hallway and bounced off every light, every door, every inch of the wall and ceiling and floor. I put my hand against the wall, steadying myself. Goose bumps pricked my arms and back. Maybe after thirteen years, someone had finally broken. Become one of them.

Alarmed at the thought, I walked down the hallway as quickly as I knew how. I reached the end and stopped. Nothing. I walked down another hallway, and then another. I passed the classrooms, their doors tightly closed, and then the exercise room, a room marked "Supply," another room with the same marking a little farther down. I had never been this far before. The exercise room was as far as I had ever gone, and yet I had only found out about that room three days ago. Walking to and from rooms in this large dome had been considered exercise enough.

I turned into another hallway and stopped. This one had a large, black door at the end of it. It didn't continue on to another hallway like the rest of them had. A reverberating shriek filled the air around me again. It was coming from behind the door, the only blackness in a sea of gray. This time, I ran.

I pulled the doorknob and flung the door wide just as the scream stopped suddenly, like it was cut in half. I blinked. The room was dark.

I felt for a light switch but there was none, so I stood there, breathing heavily, waiting for my eyes to adjust to the darkness. I heard no more screaming. I heard nothing.

Slowly, I began seeing outlines of things in the room. A blackboard on the wall next to me with no chalk in the tray. A few desks, pushed against the wall and upside down. Two were stacked on top of one another. The same gray floor and gray walls that made up every room. A classroom. But it looked like it hadn't been used in years.

I took a step inside the room and the door behind me creaked shut. I squinted and saw an opening on the far side of the classroom. A closet maybe. I stepped softly on the cold floor and stuck my head inside. Another hallway. But this one was different.

Instead of the doors with round metal doorknobs that made up every classroom, sliding doors like the ones outside of our indents were spaced apart down the hall. Three of them. And instead of the glass that fogged over and blackened when we closed our doors, these doors were clear.

And inside two of these rooms was a person.

I gasped, brought my hand over my mouth so they wouldn't hear me. They were sleeping, lying on beds that looked just like ours in rooms that were identical. And they looked just like we did.

I stopped at the first room. A male that looked around my age with dirty blond hair was lying with his hands crossed over his stomach, the blanket in a gray heap on top of him. His chest rose slowly, calmly. What was he doing here? I watched him for another minute and then turned, headed back down the hall.

If I didn't know about this, maybe no one did. We didn't keep secrets from each other. We had voted against it. I needed to tell someone. I needed to find Mr. Dabir.

"Wait!" I froze. Someone had spoken. My hands trembled as I turned around.

It was him.

His hands were pressed up against the glass, his blanket on the floor. He was looking at me. And for the first time in thirteen years, my breath was sucked out of me.

His eyes.

They were bright, brighter than I had ever seen in anyone, pools of blue with dots of yellow and green and gold. There was a depth in them, an intensity that brought back a memory I had forgotten—a memory of when my mother had taken me to the ocean. They were clear, mesmerizing. It was the first time in thirteen years that I couldn't bring myself to look away.

"Hey." His eyes were searching mine as he spoke. It made me immediately uncomfortable.

"You aren't with them, are you? Well, you are, but…" He broke off. "You don't know."

He was talking with ease, like he had done it for his entire life. I stood still, paralyzed.

"Do you know how to get me out of here?" He spoke softly this time, moved along the glass wall until he was right next to me, the sliding door in between.

I stepped away, finally found the words to speak.

"Who are you?"

The boy chuckled. *Chuckled.* That was a form of laughter, wasn't it? I had never heard such a thing. It sounded foreign to me— hollow, distant.

"I'm just like you." His eyes, still sparkling, wrinkled at the edges. His mouth curved into a smile.

There was something different about this boy. Something wrong. None of us down here knew how to smile—we only had memories. It was weird seeing it. It looked different from what I had heard. The only laughter I remembered was from them—the violent ones. I heard them shriek with laughter, saw them snicker, after they had killed my mother. But this smile seemed different.

He stuck his hand out toward me.

"My name's Lander," He chuckled again, brought his hand back to his side when he remembered there was a door between us.

"Laney?" Another voice broke through the air. It came from the end of the hallway.

It was Mr. Dabir. He was standing with one hand on the doorknob, staring at us.

"Laney, what are you doing here? You shouldn't be here."

I looked at him, then back at the boy. His face had changed. Disappointment. Anger.

"Please, you can't keep me here!" He spoke to Mr. Dabir like he knew him, like he had seen him before. Mr. Dabir tore his eyes from me and looked at the boy. At Lander. But only for a moment.

"Laney, come here." Mr. Dabir motioned for me in a way that I had never seen him before. He was frantic. Desperate.

"I'm not like him! Please, if you let me go, I can change things. Make them better. I can show you what you've been looking for." Lander was pressed against the wall, but he was standing tall. His bright blue eyes were on the teacher.

Not like who? I was standing, rooted to the ground, my eyes on Lander, when I heard it. The yell filled the room, stabbed the air like it was alive. It was the same sound I had heard before, and it was coming from the indent next to Lander's. I turned, stunned, to the man that the sound was coming from. He had been sleeping before, and he had looked just like Lander. Just like us. But when he looked back at me, a chill shook my body and rocked my bones.

His eyes were black. Lifeless. Seething with violence and anger and hate. He was one of them. One of the violent men who destroyed the world.

I blinked. No.

He turned to me, stopped screaming for a moment. His chest heaved in and out and a trail of something wet trickled down his chin. I recognized his face—that dark, choppy hair. The olive skin that was slightly orange where the edges of his cheeks met his ears. I had seen him before. But where?

"Laney, step away from Adrian now!"

I stopped. Adrian. I heard his name called every day at meals and Collaboration, saw him stand to acknowledge it time and time again. He wasn't one of them.

He was one of us.

10

I screamed and bolted up in bed.

I looked around quickly, frantically. The blanket was twisted around my legs. I blinked. My clothes were folded neatly on the bed next to mine, where I always left them before I went to sleep. My shoes were lined up next to each other against the wall. The door to my indent was closed, locked from the inside as I always had. It had all been a dream? I was trembling.

A shrill sound filled my room and I gasped, then stilled. The bell. The alarm was sounding so I would wake up. So I would join the rest of the eight and go above to a world that was once destroyed by brutality and bitterness. So I would find something peaceful about this world, something good. So I would give the people down here a reason to start life again. I thought of the black eyes and I shuddered.

No one spoke at breakfast. For one brief moment when everyone was watching their food, I turned my head. Looked for Adrian. I wasn't sure where he sat, but I wanted to try. I caught the eyes of one of the teachers and forced my head down again. The blood rushed from my hands. I didn't see him. I didn't see Adrian. What if it wasn't a dream? That would mean our world—peaceful, calm, quiet—was corrupt. That it was possible for us to turn down here. I tried to swallow, but my food was caught in my throat. We wouldn't survive. If one turned, so would the rest of us. We would all be dead.

The men with black eyes would kill us all. Adrian—Adrian could kill us all.

I put down my fork. My appetite was gone.

Nash finished within minutes. He sat at the table with round eyes until the next bell rang—the last bell we would hear until we returned.

We walked to Collaboration, all ninety-seven of us. When I stepped through the door into the dome-shaped room, Mr. Dabir was standing in the center. He motioned to us all to join him, to stand next to him. His eyes stopped on me for a moment too long, and I thought of him frantically motioning me away from Adrian. From the boy with the bright blue eyes.

Everyone was seated and silence filled the room once again. I was standing in between Nash and Alese. Theodore was on her other side.

Mr. Dabir cleared his throat.

"After the eight we have chosen return from their journey above ground, we will know without a doubt that the destruction is over, that the world above is safe to start a new life—our life. We will know that we do not need to be afraid anymore." He looked at us, then out at the people—the glassy eyes that stared back at us.

"We ask our eight to return not only with good news, but with anything they can find that is left over from a time when peace— when love—existed. We need proof that love still exists, so we can harness it once again. Then we will have the missing pieces to our foundation of peace, and we will be able to start anew."

Mr. Dabir looked at them without blinking.

"This is the only way to ensure that violence will never destroy our world again. That violent and hateful men will never again walk the earth," his voice broke, but he regained composure almost as quickly as it did. "That we will not become them."

The people were still, their eyes on Mr. Dabir and all of us. Fear and mistrust of the world above swam through their dull eyes, but they didn't seem as angry as they had been when Nash and I were chosen as part of the eight. Maybe they too were starting to believe that we could not live down here forever.

That was it. That was our send-off to the world above.

As I walked past the chairs to the door, my eyes met the eyes of an older woman. She was the one I had sat next to at breakfast a few days before. She looked back at me, her eyes clouded like the rest but different. Calmer. More at peace. And then she winked.

I stared, wondering if what I had just seen was my imagination. My mother had winked once. My mother…

The old woman's eyes left mine and she followed everyone else up the aisle, out the door, and was gone.

Everyone went to studies while the eight of us were led by Mr. Dabir out the room and down the hallway. We passed by the classrooms and the exercise room and stopped at a room labeled "Supply." I stopped for a moment, touched the wall. This seemed familiar.

Mr. Dabir took something out of his pocket. Sunglasses. He put them on and opened the door, closing it behind us. My eyes widened, and by the way the rest were standing in silence, I was sure their eyes did too.

The room was filled with things from the time before we were brought down here. Thick, bulky coats were in a pile on the ground in front of us. They were gray like the room surrounding. But the other piles—they were filled with colors we had not seen in years, aside from the colors of hair and eyes. I had almost forgotten what they were called.

Red, blue, and purple scarves were piled next to the coats. Backpacks were beside them—green, black, and yellow. Boots were stacked against the wall, with what looked like rubber soles beneath them. Lighter jackets were in the corner, from a pale blue to a soft pink.

Seeing gray for so long does something to a person. The colors seemed too bright, obnoxious even. No wonder Mr. Dabir had shaded his eyes.

"I know it's against our vote to have anything of color, but this is all we have for supplies," Mr. Dabir was looking at the colors in disdain. "Some of the teachers managed to bring them down here before we shut the doors. They will have to do. Just try not to look at them for too long."

At Mr. Dabir's insistence, we each picked out a jacket, boots, and a backpack. I lifted the straps to my shoulders, and it felt heavy.

"The backpacks are filled with supplies. It should be everything you need for a few weeks' journey."

We left the room as quickly as we had come in. The gray walls seemed calm against our bright jackets.

Mr. Dabir felt his pockets and headed back inside once he had come out.

"I forgot the key."

I stood with everyone else in the empty hallway. But I wanted to see something—to see if this hallway was not just a coincidence.

I took a few steps away from Arsen, who was standing next to me. They were all looking at the door, waiting for Mr. Dabir to come out again. From this point, I could just see the other door down the hall. My heart skipped a beat for the second time in thirteen years. The large gray door had a sign on it, just like this one. Just like in my dream.

"Supply."

The door was open barely. Whoever had filled our backpacks with things that were not in the first supply room had probably forgotten to close it.

As far as I could see, the room was filled with food. Water jugs were stacked up countlessly against the wall. It looked like enough food to last years, decades even. But Mr. Dabir had said we were running out of food—that this was why we were going above.

I heard his hand on the doorknob and I stepped back into the group, confused. He looked at us in silence.

"Okay," he finally spoke. "Follow me. And remember this route." His eyes darted past us to another hallway. "It's how you will get back to us."

11

We crossed four hallways and then went up stairs for what seemed like hours. I remember thinking that if I went up any more stairs, I would drown. We had lived on one floor for thirteen years. The air seemed to thin the higher we climbed.

Theodore was breathing heavily behind me but he didn't slow. I looked back at him and he nodded, his dull green-brown eyes clouded with worry. He had no memories of the world above, none except the memory of his mother being killed. He had no idea what he was walking into. I nodded back.

Dalia stopped in front of me, and I could see that the rest of the line had stopped too. We emptied out into a small room with stone walls and floor like the rest. But at the far side of this room, directly in front of us, was a large, square stone door, tightly closed. It filled up the entire wall; a dozen could fit through it at the same time easily.

I stopped, breathed. This was it—the only way out of here. The door to the world.

Mr. Dabir faced us, his eyes passing slowly over each one. He was silent, watching, for a full minute. Then he spoke.

"You spent thirteen years learning, growing, staying strong." His voice was firm, steady. "Do not let the world change you like they did."

Mr. Dabir put his hand on a rounded bar sticking out from the wall and grabbed it firmly with his fingers.

"If you do not return in a few weeks' time, we will vote again and send others."

Send others? I thought they had said it was not possible for the hateful men to still be living after all these years. Why wouldn't we return?

Our teacher pulled the bar down sharply and the door groaned open. Light flooded the room—blinding, white light. First in the form of a thin line on the floor and then it filled every corner, every empty space around us and within us. I covered my eyes—they were burning.

"Go!" Mr. Dabir was shielding his face from the wall of light. "Your journey begins now!"

The others had their hands over their faces, stunned. I opened my eyes and squinted. Nash was staggering forward, pushing toward the brightness. The moment he took a step outside the door it engulfed him. I could no longer see his outline. One by one, the others did the same, disappearing into the pounding glow. Only I was left. Someone shifted next to me, stepped back. No, there was one more.

I tried to see who it was, peered through the light. It was Theodore. He stood next to me, trembling, shaking his head with his hands over his face.

Mr. Dabir began to close the door.

I started to move forward but stopped, looked back. I opened my mouth and then closed it, my throat dry. The door was halfway shut. I had to assume Mr. Dabir was only going to open it once.

"Theodore!" My voice found itself before I knew what I was saying.

He looked up at me, tears brimming in his already cloudy eyes.

I hesitated, searched for words. Then I remembered something my mom had said—something she had told me when we heard the men begin to attack our town. When we had first heard the screaming.

"It's going to be okay."

Theodore looked at me once, his eyes widened. I didn't know if he had ever heard those words before. I didn't know if he even knew what they meant.

He stilled his shaking hands, put them over his forehead to shield them. Then he stepped out the door without looking back.

The door was almost closed, and I looked at Mr. Dabir one last time. His hands were still over his face, his eyes closed. The whole world was in front of him, beyond the large gray door, and he hadn't even looked.

I took a deep breath and remembered my mother, putting the picture of us cowering beneath the birds on the fireplace with what seemed like pride. I remembered Alese's story about the tree, the tree that had survived against all odds. I remembered the graying woman who had winked at me from across the audience then continued on with her day. I remembered Lander—the way he had curved his mouth to form a smile. His eyes that had been almost as bright as this light.

I stepped through just as the door closed with a thud—stepped into the world that had been demolished, devastated because of a ban on love. I stepped into the world that I had not seen in thirteen years.

12

It was everywhere. It filled my eyes like the light had just moments before. Everything was a blur, a blob of paint that stretched out before me as far as I could see. A blob of color—radiant, glistening, vivid color.

The others stood before me, motionless, staring out at the world before them. It was the world we had come from so many years ago, and yet it was everything but.

Emerald grass stretched before us in a field, a valley. Massive walls of rock in shades of deep brown and apricot bordered the valley, stretching to the sky. And the sky—it was a turquoise that faded to crimson as it blended into the sun. The sun was beaming, sparkling. Its brightness had faded because it now had the whole world to shine on.

I closed my eyes. Opened them. Closed them again. This couldn't be real. I remembered the sky, but during the last year of my life, it had been filled with black smoke. I remembered grass and rock, but not like this. Then, it was just something that was. Now, it seemed more than that. It was staggering.

I held my breath as I watched the movement of air, the wind, as it was once called, pass through everything, touch it, leave it quivering in its path. The grass swayed softly. A pebble fell from the cliff, echoing as it bounced onto the ground.

The world—it was not destroyed. It had grown and learned to survive even after all that had happened to it. Even after it had been scraped up and thrown into a pile. The people that had succumbed to violence must be long gone by now. They would never let something like this—the grass, the clear blue sky—remain.

I wondered for a moment if the others were still staring. I couldn't bring myself to look away. All this time we had been living underground, and this had been on top of us for who knows how many years. A perfect world.

I heard pounding on the door behind me and jumped. Mr. Dabir?

I turned, saw that most of the other eight had turned to look too.

It was Arsen. He beat his fists against the door that was now closed—the door that now led to another world. Our world underground.

"Mr. Dabir! Let me in!" Arsen screamed the words, desperate. I braced, uneasy. What had he seen?

"Arsen." Mallory walked up to him.

He turned to her, his hands over his eyes.

"The colors. The sun. It's too much." He was breathing quickly, rapidly. "I can't look at it for this long. I can't."

He put his palms on the door and let them slide down, slowly. He stopped, took a few deep breaths. Then he took his backpack off, threw it in front of him. He reached inside and pulled out a pair of dark sunglasses and slipped them on his head. They looked like the sunglasses Mr. Dabir had worn in the supply room.

Nash was looking at Arsen, his eyes unreadable. Gavin was next to him, arms crossed over his chest. I watched as Arsen zipped his backpack and stood up, breathed, looked forward through his shades. He had been the first in the exercise room to say he was ready, and now that we were here, he was the first to want to go back.

"We need to go," Gavin spoke, his eyes still on Arsen. He turned and walked into the grass, into the green field. We followed slowly.

We didn't know where we were going, just that we had to go. We had to go not too far, but far enough—far enough that we made sure the world was safe, and far enough that we discovered the secret of peace. The secret of this thing they called love.

We walked through the field together, the grass rustling under our feet. The breeze swept through my hair and up into the sky. I breathed deeply. I had never felt air so clear before, so easy to breathe.

Nash was walking in front of me when he stopped. He reached down, grabbed a handful of grass, and placed it in a pocket in his backpack. He must have wanted to show it to the others underground—to prove that the world we would talk about did exist. It was a piece of the world before destruction, and we had been told to bring as much of it back as we could.

Mallory looked back at Nash after he stopped, her hands shielded over her eyes. It wasn't just Arsen. The colors were difficult for her to look at too.

We reached the end of the field and came to a long, grassy slope. I clung to the straps of my backpack and started up it. Maybe we would be able to see more of the world from the top of the slope.

Gavin was leading the way, followed by Nash, Alese, Dalia, myself, Theodore, Mallory, and then Arsen. We had all walked one after another in the hallways for so long that it just seemed natural, even out here.

While we walked, I looked at the ground, at the grass that bent gently beneath my feet. I thought of the grass that had once been by our house before it was burned, next to the field of wildflowers. I hadn't seen any flowers yet.

For a moment I wondered if my house was close by. What was left of my house. None of us remembered how far we had come to get to the Dome, our home underground. Each of us had been brought when violence was at its peak in our towns, so we had all come in chaos, walked through streets of fire and confusion. For all we knew, we could have walked for hours or for days.

Suddenly Dalia shrieked, pointed toward the sky.

"What is that? What is that!"

I looked up, reaching for my backpack at the same time. The only weapons we had been given were a knife each, from the place where the food was prepared. The Dome had no other weapons, as a precaution. From our experience before the Dome, a weapon in the hands of man was a dangerous thing. But out here, in case we came across anything threatening, it was necessary, Mr. Dabir had told us. We needed to survive so we could return to the others.

Gavin looked alarmed, his knife already in his hand, pointed to the sky. Theodore's eyes were wide, filled with fear. But Alese was looking up with a calmness in her eyes. It almost looked as though her mouth curved slightly, like the boy in my dream.

Then I saw it, let go of the breath I had been holding.

It was a bird.

Nash looked at Dalia, an expression of questioning on his face. He was wondering if she was serious, if she really didn't know. She looked back at him.

"I said what is that? Will it hurt us?"

Nash opened his mouth, closed it again. He looked at Alese and she spoke, her eyes still on the feathered body soaring through the turquoise air.

"It's a bird," she said it softly, almost whispered it. She was thinking the same thing I was. Birds still existed? They had found a way to survive the destruction too.

Dalia did not look satisfied. She opened her mouth but Theodore spoke first.

"What's a bird?"

Alese looked at Theodore, then back at the bird.

"It's like us." She paused, thinking back on some distant memory. "But it knows how to fly."

13

We set up camp when we reached the top of the grassy slope, laid out blankets before the sky turned dark.

We had no firewood, didn't even know if wood still existed because we hadn't seen any trees. But we were told it was the warm season before we came above ground, so we weren't cold.

The top of the slope had given us a view of another piece of the world: a long, downward slope that melted into more fields filled with grass. The grass ended what looked like miles away at the base of a huge, rocky slope, thirty times higher than the slope we had just climbed. A mountain, Nash had called it. He said that his town had been on a landmark similar to what lay before us, and that was the name his people used.

He, Alese, and I seemed to know the most about this world, about the world before everything became ruin. I was the last of us to have been brought underground, so it made sense. I had more time for memories and more years before the destruction hit us. They must have been brought underground shortly before I was. And the rest—Dalia, Theodore, Gavin, Mallory, and Arsen—the violence must have reached their towns first. For them, ashes and black sky were all they remembered. That, and fear. Danger.

Nash was leaning against his backpack next to me, his eyes on the mountain in the distance. He was lost in thought, probably thinking of what his life used to be like before he went to the

Dome. Trying to remember, and trying not to forget. For all he knew, that mountain could be his.

Arsen was on his other side, laying his blanket on the ground, picking it up again, and then laying it another way. He finally huffed, threw his backpack on top of it, and lay down. Mallory was trying to fluff out her backpack next to him, make it more comfortable so she could use it as a pillow. Dalia was doing the same. Theodore and Alese were on their backs, staring at the sky.

The turquoise had melted into a light blue that faded, slowly, into a deep violet color at the edges. The sun had turned crimson, like fire. It was slipping away, breath by breath, heading to the end of the earth. And then it dropped beneath the horizon and the sky turned black. It seemed to pause. Little pockets of light began appearing in the blanket of darkness, dim at first, and then brighter. There were thousands of them. They filled the sky and made the darkness not as dark anymore—not as colorless. It was something even I had trouble remembering. During the five years that I had lived in this world, we had voted against going outside at night because we were never sure when the destruction would reach us.

The others seemed taken, mesmerized, like they were looking at night for the first time too. The ceiling of the Dome had been black, like the sky that had once been filled with smoke. It was nothing like this.

Theodore put his hands behind his head, his eyes still on the dots of light. It almost looked like they were winking, like my mother had. Like the old woman from the Dome.

"Tell me," he breathed, his eyes fixed above. "Tell me more about this world."

His only memory of his life before he moved underground really was his mother being killed. I almost felt sorry for him. But I didn't know how to feel sorry for someone. None of us did.

Gavin was lying in the grass, his blanket rolled up beneath his head, and he sat up, looked at Theodore.

"I remember screaming, people dying, my mother hiding me in a closet and seeing her slaughtered when men came in to kill us."

He was angry, his eyes in slits. "She was terrified, pleaded for her life, but no, that wasn't enough, didn't mean anything to them. I remember a sky that was so thick with smoke people died because they couldn't breathe. Houses torn apart and left in a pile. Is that the world you're talking about?"

Gavin looked at Theodore one more time and then lay back down and folded his arms.

He didn't remember anything good about the world. No wonder his eyes always looked darker than the rest.

Silence filled the air. Theodore hadn't moved, hadn't taken his eyes from the sky.

Dalia shifted slightly, adjusting her blond bun beneath her head.

"That story I told at Collaboration—about my grandmother clapping after I had learned the difference between the herbs—that wasn't true." She stopped, traced her hand on her blanket. "I never had a grandmother. She died before I was born."

She hesitated. "I…I clapped once. I guess it was one of the first things I did when I was a baby. I don't remember—my mother told me about it right before the violence overtook our town. She said I had clapped, that's what she called it, and never to do it again. That I would be a target for the dangerous people. That if they saw me do it, they would want to kill me before anyone else." Dalia shook her head, her voice softened. "It didn't matter. They killed her anyway, and they would have killed me too."

Then she sat up, her voice strengthened, and she looked at all of us.

"But that meant it was good, right? From the time before the destruction, the time of peace? Why else would those people hate it?"

No one answered, but no one denied it either. That must have been enough for Dalia. She lay back down in silence.

"And what about you, Laney?" My heart jumped when I heard my name. Nash was turning on his backpack, looking at me. "I don't think any of us know anything about you."

I swallowed, looked back at him. His blue eyes, dark from the night, didn't look away. I lowered my eyes. I had to speak. He wasn't going to turn away until I did.

"I was five." I looked up, hoping to get some sort of comfort from the night sky. A breeze swept through us, raising the hair on my arms. "Before that day, I remember rivers crashing against rocks and rising from the sweat of the sand. I remember the sun sliding farther down the sky each night, stepping over clouds and the red of the air to seek a destination that is never permanent. I remember fields of wildflowers stretching their heads toward the sky and drinking in the last bit of warmth from the sun."

I stopped. Others had turned. They were looking at me too. I took a breath, the field of bright yellow flowers filling my memories.

"I remember watching them each night and wondering why, with their heads turned toward the sun and their chubby stalks firmly in the ground, they were trembling. When I heard gunshots and I saw my mother crumple into the wildflowers, I never wondered again."

For a second, I thought I saw sadness fill Nash's eyes. He never looked away.

I didn't move. I felt the wind; an insect chirped somewhere far away.

I looked at the clouds at the edge of the sky, but somewhere deep in my mind, they reminded me of the thick, black smoke that used to smother the air. I thought of the yellow wildflowers, of the way they used to stare at the sun. But as quickly as they filled my mind, an image of my mother, dying, took their place.

I couldn't help but think that maybe this journey above ground was for nothing. Maybe when love left someone, it never returned. Maybe none of us could be fixed.

14

When light began to smother the black sky, we packed up our things and stood at the top of the slope, staring at the world below.

A thin, dense cloud covered the area around us so all we saw was white. White above us, white below us. It was like the colors had taken a break to appear in some other part of the world.

Theodore was standing next to me, his arms wrapped around his chest.

"How do we know which way to go if we can't see?"

We had always been able to see. In the hallways in the gray Dome, in our classrooms. Even in the world before we went underground, nothing had blocked our view like this. I was confused; I had never seen such a thing.

Nash walked forward, his arms stretched out, running his fingers through the cloud like it was water.

"It's fog. A cloud that comes down on the world but then goes back up again."

Gavin looked at him and Nash shrugged.

"We used to see it all the time on our mountain."

Conversation had become more frequent now, almost common. It was something about this world. We came here, and the others had started to believe it was normal. Or maybe they believed everything we were saying to each other was necessary, like Mr. Dabir had allowed. Either way, it was amazing how easily they all seemed to catch on to it again. After thirteen years of near-silence, it felt strange. Too loud.

"So I guess we can either wait here until it goes away, or try to find our way down in it," Gavin said, his eyes peering into the whiteness.

Theodore stared silently ahead. Arsen adjusted the sunglasses on his head that he had been wearing since yesterday. Dalia looked at Gavin.

Nash let out a breath and swept his eyes around the circle once. "Let's take a vote."

A vote. Like Collaboration. It was something that had always seemed to keep the peace in the past, and it was what we knew. For a second, I found myself agreeing with Nash. Approving of his idea. It was the first thing that seemed normal since we had come out here. Like home.

Nash looked to his left. Dalia. She fumbled for a moment, caught off guard. But then she regained her composure and tightened her bun.

"I vote we keep going. We aren't accomplishing anything by staying up here."

Nash nodded and looked at Mallory.

"I vote the same."

Arsen.

"Yes. Let's just get this trip over with."

Alese was next. She looked out at the fog with wide eyes.

"I vote to keep going too."

Gavin was watching everyone with narrowed eyes.

"Fine. Whatever."

Nash looked at me. I nodded.

"I vote the same."

Theodore was last. He looked out at the fog, looked back at us, and then looked out again. He wrapped his arms around himself again. I could see worry in his eyes.

"Okay," he unwrapped his arms and grabbed the straps of his backpack. "I vote with you guys."

Nash looked at all of us again and nodded.

"Let's go then."

I let out a breath I was holding. All of us had agreed. That was good. In the Dome, everyone had to agree for something to be put into motion. Any disagreements meant nothing happened. I didn't know what we would do if we hadn't all voted the same.

Nash led the way as we started down the slope, the fog surrounding us. I had wondered once, when I was a child, what it would be like to be inside a cloud. I had been lying in the field of flowers, staring up at the sky. It was a pointless thing to have wondered that, I thought now. Because now I knew.

We had only been walking for a few minutes when I heard someone ahead of me cry out. It was louder, but then muffled as it moved away through the fog. It seemed to have moved away too fast. Were they running? There was another shout, from someone else, Dalia maybe. And then another.

I slowed and opened my mouth to call out to them, to ask what was up there. None of us could see each other; the cloud was too thick. But when I took another step, there was no ground beneath me.

My heart hit my throat as I dropped into the air and fell onto something below. The ground around me was soft again, damp. The grassy slope. But what—?

I tried to grab a handful of the grass but I couldn't. The ground was slippery and the slope was steeper than it had been, much steeper. I couldn't stop.

I slid down the hill at a pace much faster than I ever remembered going. The air rushed past me and cooled my cheeks and my ears, chilling me to the bone. The wind was screaming. Terror filled my mind, but for a brief moment it turned into something else—I felt…exhilarated. Alive. The feeling disappeared as soon as it had come and the terror was back. The fog enveloped everything I could have seen, the white sheet tightly closed, taunting, daring me to find the opening. And then I did.

I slid out of the world of white and into a world of color once again. I saw Nash, Alese, and Dalia at the bottom of the slope, brushing grass off their clothes. The slope leveled out quickly and my body slowed, coming to a stop just feet from them. My breathing had quickened and my fingers were white. I stilled my shaking hands and closed my eyes. I was still lying on the grass when Nash spoke.

"Well, that's a way to get down a hill, isn't it? Who wants to go again?"

Again? I opened my eyes and he was looking at me. I looked back. It could have been the sun, but I thought his eyes looked a little brighter. The gray-brown they had once been was now less gray and more brown. His face was flushed, his cheeks red. His skin had color now, not just his clothes. I blinked. As soon as I saw it, it was gone. His eyes clouded over.

"Again?" Dalia looked at Nash in disbelief, mirroring my thoughts. "That was terrifying. I'm just glad I'm alive."

The rest of the eight came sliding down the slope as we had, eyes wide and breathing fast. Mallory was last in the group, so last to fall. She was screaming, her hands wrapped around her head as she slid down the grass. When she came to a stop, she looked at us, then at Nash, her mouth wide open.

"This was your fault. You had us take a vote! We should have just stayed up there." She stood hastily and turned away, her arms brushing her shirt and hair.

"Mallory," Arsen said.

"Don't talk to me!" Mallory continued to brush the grass off, checking to see if she was hurt in any way.

Nash just looked at her.

Theodore was staring back up at the slope we had just come from, the fog still wrapped around the top like something I remembered in the past. Something white, and cold. I couldn't think of the name. I followed his gaze and then looked back at him. Something red was running down his arm and staining his shirt.

"Theodore," I breathed his name, pointed to his arm.

Dalia gasped and Nash stepped toward him to get a better view. Theodore tore his eyes from the slope and looked back at me, then down at his arm. At the blood.

He held out his hand for Nash to stop, wiped the blood away with his hand.

"Don't," he spoke softly. Then he looked back up at the grass, at the fog. His eyes turned to us once again.

"I didn't…" He paused, searching for the words. "I didn't hate that."

We all stood silent for a moment, staring. Then Nash answered him, the sun casting a hint of yellow into his eyes.

"Fun." Theodore looked at him, confused. Nash nodded. "I think the word you're looking for is fun."

15

I stared at Nash. Everyone did. We waited. Fun? I searched my memories. If I had heard of the word before, I couldn't remember it.

Nash picked his backpack off the ground and swung it onto his shoulders.

"Let's go. The world's not coming to us."

And then he was off, like he hadn't said a thing.

Mallory threw her hands up and looked at Arsen before she picked up her backpack as well.

"This world's making him crazy."

We all started to follow. Theodore zipped his pack and tied something around his arm, where the blood had been. It was soft and frayed at the ends. A piece of his blanket. He looked at the fog one more time and then walked in the direction Nash was going.

Nash was at the end of the field when he stopped for a moment, staring at what was before him. Then he turned around quickly and yelled at the rest of us.

"Hey guys! Take a look at this!"

He disappeared beneath the field. There must have been another slope, blocking our view of him. I walked at the same pace I had been. At least we weren't going to fall this time.

I was the last to reach the end of the field, right behind Alese. She was still stopped, still staring ahead. I looked at her, her light brown bun facing me. Then I looked beyond her, and I saw it.

I sucked my breath in. It was water.

A huge blue-green circle of water was about a hundred feet before us, stretching out to the tips of the mountains. I didn't know how we had missed it before. The sun was touching it, spreading across the surface and creating a pool of turquoise light. Like the sky. The mountains reflected from the earth into the water, the purples and browns mixing with the blues and greens. It looked like another world, one that you could simply dive into and never return.

Alese was quiet next to me, and then she turned. There was a tear in her eye, and she brushed it away.

"My town was by water like this." She looked back at the blue that filled the world before us. "It looks just like it."

I looked back out at the scene before us and saw Nash, halfway between us and the water. He was running. He dropped his backpack on the grass and threw his hands up into the air as he reached the edge of the water and jumped into it—jumped into the blue world.

I looked behind him, confused. No one was chasing him. He wasn't trying to go after something, like I had in my dream. He was just running. Running because he wanted to, and running because he could.

I looked back at Alese and her eyes had brightened, her mouth had taken the shape it had when she first saw the bird. Then she ran after him, her jacket in her hand flailing behind her, stopping when she reached the edge of the water. She knelt down and touched the water with her hand, then splashed it over her face.

The rest of us were watching them in disbelief. Gavin was walking slowly toward the water with his arms folded, and Mallory and Arsen followed at a safe distance. I saw Mallory say something to Arsen, her eyes on Nash, and he nodded. I walked behind them, slowly, feeling the grass beneath my feet.

When I was a few feet from the pool, I saw Nash get out and ring the water from the bottom of his shirt. It was wet, and it clung to his skin. It clung to his stomach, outlining the muscles beneath. He looked over at me and saw that my eyes were on him.

I took a breath and looked away quickly. We all had loose clothes for a reason. Jealousy. Lust.

I turned my eyes back to the body of water that stood before me. It was massive, overwhelming. My town had been in a valley, one with rocks and grass and dirt, much like the one we had stepped into when we came through the door into this world. No one ever traveled farther than to the town that was closest to you, to get food and clothes. I had never even done that; I never left. I didn't even know something like this existed.

I stepped up to the water's edge and looked across it, to the mountains. Then I passed my eyes over the surface, running them over the length of the huge pool, from the mountains to me. When my eyes reached the water below me, I stopped. I saw a person on the blue surface, someone who wasn't a part of the eight.

I panicked, looked behind me, and braced for whoever was there. At least it was a girl, and it didn't look like her eyes were black. At least not yet. Nash was watching me and I looked at him, opened my mouth to tell him what I had seen. But then I stopped. He wasn't telling me something, I could see it in his eyes.

"Laney." He gestured to the water in front of him, where a sandy blond-haired, brown-eyed boy stared back at him. Then he looked at me.

"It's you."

My breath left me as I looked where he was pointing. At the girl. It was a reflection. My hands trembled. It was a reflection of *me*.

A girl with brown hair pulled into a bun and brown eyes stared back at me from the water. Her face was an oval shape that made her eyes look large, her eyelashes were long and brown, like the rest. Wisps of hair cascaded from the bun and framed her face. Her cheeks were pale, flushed just barely. Her chin was strong, held high. She looked confident, but had no reason to be. I brought my hand up to my face. Touched it. The girl in the water did too. My mouth parted, I took a step back without realizing it.

This girl was me.

I looked back at the face in the water, at my eyes. They were a deep brown, clouded over by a gray color. They weren't as dark as Gavin's or Arsen's, but they were dull. Not brightened like Nash's had been. I breathed again. At least they weren't black.

Nash was still watching me, and he looked back into the water, looked back at the reflection of himself.

"Crazy, isn't it?" he spoke softly, almost in disbelief. "We haven't seen ourselves in thirteen years."

I looked around the water and saw that the rest were at the edge, looking at themselves, like I had, seeing what they looked like for the first time in years. And for some of them who didn't have memories, they were seeing themselves for the first time in their lives.

I looked back at the girl in the water without moving. Then I pulled the bun from my head, letting my light brown hair cascade around my shoulders. I don't know why I did it—don't know what made me let my hair down for the first time in thirteen years. But when I did, the girl in the water, staring back at me, seemed to brighten for just a moment. Her eyes were not as dark as they had been before. She almost looked like I imagined I did when I was a child—running to the house when my mother called, my hair twirling with the wind and my dress streaming out behind me.

I looked at her, and she looked back at me from another world, a world of blues and greens and purples. And for a moment—just a moment—I thought I saw her smile.

16

We voted to sleep by the water that night. It was a way for us to refill our water supply, Nash had said. But there was more, something that no one was saying. Something peaceful about it. Something none of us had ever felt before.

I didn't put my hair back up. I didn't know why—just felt that the girl in the turquoise water wouldn't want me to.

Alese had pulled her hair down too. It was long, and it cascaded down her back like the ripples of the water. She had dipped her head in, drenching it, and then let it dry in the sun.

Dalia seemed more taken with her reflection than anyone else. The sun was slipping slowly beneath the white wisps in the sky and she was still sitting on the edge of the lake, staring at the water below. Staring at herself.

I unzipped my backpack and took out the blanket I had rolled up and stuffed inside the night before. I flicked it once, letting it unravel with the wind, and then lay it down next to everyone else's.

Silence filled the air tonight, and I breathed deeply. The water was fading with the sun, as if the only thing that brought it life was the light. When darkness rushed in and the specks of light peered between the blackness, the water mirrored it. It was like there were two skies, sparkling with a thousand pinpricks of light. One above us, and one below us. Like we were in between worlds.

"This is surreal," Alese spoke, her voice drifting with the wind. "It's like I'm back home."

Nash was lying on his back, his elbows propped up and his eyes on the mountains at the edge of the lake.

"I know. I feel close too."

Silence filled the black sky again. Then Arsen let out a breath, louder than it needed to be. He sat up, looked at them through his sunglasses. I found myself wondering why he needed them at night.

"We get it. This world feels like home to you guys. Well, my home is the Dome. And it always will be."

Nash sat up, looked at the guy with the black hair and strong hands. What color were his eyes? I didn't remember.

"Arsen. We're not living there anymore. That's why we're here. This," he spread his arms out, looked out to the mountains again. "This is going to be our home."

Arsen snorted, his mouth twisted into a frown.

"This world is hideous. Disgusting. Unlivable." His eyes fell on the water, on Dalia. "I don't know what you see in it. But I see nothing."

Nash's eyes widened, his mouth opened. He stood to his feet.

"You see nothing? Open your eyes, Arsen. Maybe if you gave this world a chance instead of cowering beneath those sunglasses…"

His hands were trembling, but his voice was calm. Steady.

Arsen stood slowly, his eyes on Nash.

"Let's do something."

Another voice cut in quickly. Theodore. His eyes were round as he looked back and forth between Nash and Arsen. He didn't want this to happen as much as I didn't.

Nash looked at him, stopped. He wiped his hands on his pants and then sat down. I breathed again. Alese dropped her hands to her lap next to me. She had placed them on the ground, bracing herself to stand. I hadn't realized it until now.

"Let's do something," Theodore spoke softly now, like he wasn't sure what to say next. His mouth opened and closed, then opened again. He had an idea.

"A competition. Like what we did in our studies."

Nash looked at Arsen one more time, then brought his eyes slowly back to Theodore.

"Okay. What competition?"

Theodore fiddled with the zipper on his backpack.

"The Word Competition. But with something else. Because we don't have our books."

The Word Competition. Something we had done in our classroom to keep our minds sharp. We each said a word that began with a certain letter, one after another, until someone stumbled, couldn't think of another word. That someone would have to study our writing book for an hour longer than everyone else that day. Mr. Dabir had said this was the only acceptable competition that existed, because it made us smarter. Other competitions only brought people down, he had explained. In this, the objective was to learn, and the punishment was to learn. It worked. No one got any more than anyone else.

"Names," Alese spoke, sitting up straighter. "Instead of words, let's say names. Names of people we lived with in the Dome."

Names? I wondered why Alese would request that, of all things. We never talked to them. And yet we heard their names each day, several times, as they were checked into meals and Collaboration. We should know them, I realized.

"Yes, names." Theodore looked at Alese, relieved. She nodded at him gently.

"Okay, I'm in," Nash said, shrugging off his jacket and laying it on the ground next to him. "And the stakes? What happens to the person who stumbles first?"

Theodore looked at the dusty ground.

"They have to write all the names we say in the dirt. Twice."

"No," Gavin spoke for the first time, rolling over from his position where he had been looking away from us, out into the night. "They have to jump in the water."

Theodore looked at Gavin, his eyes wide. Nash looked at him too, and then his eyes fell on Arsen. He shrugged.

"Let's begin."

I blinked, looking at the rest as they darkened under the sky. There had never been an actual punishment before. No one gained anything by jumping into the lake. You always needed to gain something by it to make it okay. To make it acceptable. Didn't you?

"Laney."

I looked at Nash. He looked at Gavin. He wasn't saying my name. He was starting the competition.

"Mr. Dabir." Gavin went after him without missing a beat.

"Ms. Geena." Alese gathered her hair in her hands and threw it behind her shoulders.

Theodore took a breath, but answered quickly.

"Delma."

Everyone stared at him.

"The old woman with the gray hair," he explained.

Nash nodded. I swallowed. The woman who had winked at me, her name was Delma.

"Mallory," Arsen said it without hesitating, his voice firm.

My turn.

"Nash."

I wanted to do to him what he had done to me. So he could see what it felt like. He looked at me, his mouth curving slightly at the edges. Then he turned to Mallory.

"Theodore." Mallory seemed remotely uninterested in the competition, but she had spoken.

Round two. Nash went again.

"Anna."

I didn't know her, but I remembered her name being called at Collaboration the day we all tried to prove that we knew the most about the world with love. The day I was touched. A breeze passed over the lake and into our circle, and I wrapped my arms around myself. It seemed so long ago. Another world.

"Arsen," Gavin spoke.

"Dalia," Alese said the girl's name and looked at her, sitting on the water's edge, at the same time.

"Alese." Theodore looked down, smoothed his blanket as he said her name.

Arsen stared, unblinking.

"Gavin."

I was next. I searched for names, but I could think of none. The eight of us had already been said. The two teachers. What was another name? I searched my mind frantically. A few seconds passed in silence.

"I think we have our jumper."

Gavin looked at me and then lay back on his blanket, his hands behind his head.

My heart sunk. I looked at the others in silence. And then I stood.

"Laney. You don't have to." Nash was looking at me, his brown eyes wide.

"Yes she does," Arsen cut in. "It's all part of the competition. All part of life. She knows that."

I took a deep breath, looked at Arsen. His eyes were hidden behind his sunglasses. We had always done what we agreed to do in the Dome. Agreeing to something and then not doing it is what made the people turn violent. It's what made them who they were. Arsen was right.

I saw regret pass through Nash's eyes—like he wished he had never agreed to Gavin's conditions. I didn't understand. I had lost, not him.

I looked out at the water, at the blackness that was riddled with light. I couldn't give myself a chance to think any longer.

I ran, just as Nash had earlier, and just as Alese had done with her jacket flowing in the wind. My hair caught the air and lifted behind me. And as I was running, I felt something. It was a warmth that started in my stomach and spread out to my arms, nothing like I had felt when I ran in my dream. And for a second, I understood why they ran—why they had rushed at the water when they first saw it. I almost lifted my arms like I had seen Nash do. Almost.

I reached the edge of the black pool and jumped into the air. Just before I hit the water, I saw Dalia's face. She was looking at me, confused, like I was crazy. Maybe I was.

I hit the water and the warmth was gone in an instant. Cold flooded my fingers and arms, my hair suddenly felt heavy. I felt the ground beneath the pool and pushed. My head broke the surface and I gasped, sucked in air. My entire body was shaking.

I saw Nash and Alese at the water's edge, staring out at me, their eyes flooded with something. Something I couldn't recognize. Worry, maybe.

They watched me push myself from the water and onto the dirt next to it. Onto the grass. I sat there for a moment, and then Nash was by my side.

"Laney. Are you okay?"

The words my mother had said to me, and the words I had said to Theodore. I wondered who had said them to Nash in the past, in his life before the Dome.

I nodded, wiping the water from my face. My hair was dripping. I tried to still the shaking, but I couldn't.

"Wait here." Nash stood up and ran back to the others. If they had watched me jump, they were all looking away now, their minds on other things.

Nash hurried back, his face flushed. He held his blanket in his hand.

I looked at him, confused. I guess he was cold too.

He looked down at it, then back at me. Then down at it again.

"Here." Nash held the blanket out to me. It was white, with blue-and-green stripes, like the water. I just stared at him. I didn't understand.

"You can...use it tonight." He was still looking at me, still holding it out. "You need it more than I do."

I hesitated. Then he unwrapped the blanket, dropped it around my shoulders. He looked at me one more time, his eyes clear, searching. Like he didn't understand what he was doing, either.

He walked back to the others and I sat there, staring out at the lake, the blanket still wrapped around me. No one had ever given anything to me. No one but my mother. That was the law though. This…I didn't know what this was. I didn't know why anyone would want to give me something. Why anyone would want to be cold all night just so I could be warm.

I walked back to the eight when the sky was as dark as the world around it. Dalia was with them now. She lay on her side, her face turned away from me. Nash was on his back in the grass, his eyes closed.

I sat and looked at him for a long moment—his chest rising and falling with the wind, his hair tangled on his head. It was the color of the wildflowers.

Then I unwrapped the blanket from my shoulders and placed it on top of him before I fell asleep under the sky.

17

The next morning we woke to birds chirping. It was distant, and for a moment I thought it was coming from my dreams.

I opened my eyes and sunlight pooled in. I was almost getting used to how much brighter it was in this world than in the Dome.

Nash was already awake and sitting at the edge of the water, looking out over the reflection of the sky. His backpack was on his back, his blanket gone. He had already packed it up.

The others stirred and slowly put their things in their backpacks, stood, and stretched. We refilled our water once more before we started to walk.

It was decided. Today, we were going to the mountains. We would climb the tallest mountain and look out at the world behind it. If what we saw was like everything we had seen so far, we would turn back, head back to the Dome, and tell the others that it was safe. End our journey. If the world behind the mountains was not destroyed, then we had gone far enough. And finding proof of love? Well, if we didn't find it in the time it took for us to reach the top of the mountain, we would probably never find it. We were a few days into this world, and we had seen no trace of it yet.

I walked at the back of the eight. I still didn't understand what had happened last night, what Nash had done. I didn't want to try to understand.

The eight of us walked around the body of water and reached the base of the mountain when the sun was straight up in the sky.

We stopped to eat, looking up at what lay before us. It seemed huge, the very peak of it touching the clouds. Touching the sky. I wondered how long it would take to climb it.

We started up the rocky slope in silence, Nash leading the way. The mountains had been on his mind ever since we saw them, I knew that much. He wanted to see if these mountains were his.

I breathed, looked at the ground as I stepped. I had never heard of mountains in the past, but I imagined they'd have trees. We still hadn't seen any; these were bare. They were all rock—sharp edges stuck together with dirt sprinkled over them.

"Guys," Theodore was breathing heavily in front of me, moving slower than the rest. "I don't know if I can do this."

He stopped and put his arms on his hips, breathed in deeply. He was looking up, at the peak of the mountain. He had never done something this challenging, had never even seen a mountain before we came to this world. And now here he was, climbing it, like it was the most normal thing in the world.

"Come on!" Nash yelled from the front of the pack, his voice distant. "The world's not coming to us!"

Those words again.

I looked at Theodore and he looked back at me. I nodded. He could do this. We had to.

He drew in a deep breath and turned, started up the mountain again.

An hour passed as we walked, the rocks crunching beneath our feet. My hair was damp, and I pushed it behind my neck.

The sun was drifting down the sky when the rock slid beneath me and I stumbled. I put my hands out to brace myself as I fell, landing on the dirt. I stayed there for a second, breathing. The rocks were sharp, but I was fine. Nothing had been hurt.

Then I froze, my stomach tightening. The ground in front of me was brown, rocky, like the rest of the mountain. But to the right of my hand, behind some small rocks and in the dirt, was a flower.

A flower.

It was rooted to the ground, with a thin green stem and petals that trembled in the wind. It was yellow, a deep yellow that faded at the edges into a milky cream color. Just like my flowers. Just like the flowers my mother had been killed in.

"Hey! Wait a second!" Theodore yelled it to the rest of the group. He must have seen me fall.

An image of my mother flooded my mind. She had heard the screaming, ran down the wooden steps of the house with her apron wrapped tightly around her waist because she knew I was playing in the wildflowers. She called out my name, searched the yellow stalks frantically with her eyes. Only then did they see her. Hear her. The men. The gunshot sounded in my mind and I saw fear flash through her blue eyes before they clouded over and she fell, crushing the flowers beneath her. She wouldn't have been killed if I hadn't been playing in the wildflowers. If I had stayed inside, like I should have been, she would still be here today. The flowers were the reason she wasn't here.

I sucked in my breath, stared at the flower before me. I looked around it. There were no other flowers; a rocky surface made up the rest of the ground. How the flower had grown up here, survived up here, I didn't know. But flowers still existed. That, I did know.

The eight had stopped, were looking back at me from their places on the mountain. I saw Nash look at me and then follow where my gaze had been—at the flower.

I stood up, brushed my hands on my pants and adjusted my shirt. "I'm fine. Let's go."

Nash looked at me again, his eyes unreadable. He hadn't moved.

Arsen grabbed onto the straps of his backpack and looked at Nash, waited for him to move.

"She said she's fine. Let's go."

Nash hesitated again but then turned slowly, started walking back up the mountain. The others followed.

Theodore looked at me and then at my hands, for blood maybe. "Laney?"

His eyes were wide, questioning. He knew something was wrong. That it was more than just falling.

I breathed, shaking the memories from my mind. I hoped that was the only flower that remained. That all the rest had been destroyed.

"Come on." I looked at Theodore, nodding forward. He looked back at me and then turned and started up the mountain again.

I started climbing and then stopped one more time. Turned. The flower was bending slightly in the wind. I turned forward, up the mountain, up the layers of rock and dirt. I didn't look back.

18

The sky was turning a deep blue that melted into purples and reds when Nash finally stopped climbing. It was a semi-flat area with more dirt than rocks scattered on the ground—at least we would have as few sharp stones digging into our backs as possible.

A breeze passed over the mountain and swept beneath our blankets, ruffling them after we had laid them down. I shivered and zipped my jacket to my neck. I looked up. Dalia and Alese had put their jackets on too.

"I'm going to go see if I can find something—a big rock, dead grass, I don't know—anything we can use to start a fire," Nash spoke, watching as Theodore pulled his jacket out of his backpack too. "It gets colder on mountains at night."

Nash swung his backpack on his back and turned, started to walk around the side of the mountain.

No one questioned him. I watched him disappear from view and then bent down and brushed the rocks from the ground right in front of me. Theodore grabbed his blanket that he had laid in a bundle next to Arsen's and walked over, laid it down next to me.

"Do you think he'll be okay? Out there by himself?"

I looked at Theodore. His red hair had grown a little bit from the standard short haircut that every male had in the Dome. His green eyes were round, like they always seemed to be.

"Yeah." I looked away from him, smoothed my blanket out on the dirt. "I think he can handle himself pretty well."

Theodore's face brightened for a moment and he sat down on his backpack. The wind blew again and lifted his blanket into the air, but he had shoved a corner of it underneath the weight of his backpack, so it stayed in place.

I paused as I spread my blanket out again, putting the end of it under my backpack as he had done. I looked again at the boy next to me, only a few years younger, but years that had made all the difference in memories. He was looking out at the view of the water below, now a smaller pool that was fading with the sun. The field spread after that, and then the long, grassy slope.

There was something about Theodore—a simplicity that no one else in the group seemed to have. An innocence. I remembered Collaboration, the red-haired boy that stood in front of the people with his eyes down and his hands trembling. His mouth open, the noise filling the air and bouncing off the gray walls. The noise that seemed to reach down inside of me and squeeze my heart.

"Theodore." I found myself saying his name before the thought drifted from my mind.

He looked up at me and his eyes brightened again. Brightened because I had said his name. A strand of hair fell over my forehead and I tucked it behind my ear.

"That noise you made, at Collaboration." I took a breath and my heartbeat quickened. "What was that?"

Theodore's eyes faded some and he looked down, fidgeted with the edge of his blanket.

"She called it…" He stopped. Looked back up at me. His eyes suddenly looked deep, pools of green and blue, like the water below us. He brought the corners of his mouth up slightly. "She called it singing."

Then he looked down again, stared at the blanket like it was a memory he was trying to grasp, trying not to forget.

I suddenly wondered why I had asked him. Why I had brought back that memory, his only memory. I wanted to comfort him, wanted to put my hand on his shoulder. I blinked, shook the thoughts from my head. What was I thinking? Touch was forbidden.

I wrapped my jacket around me more tightly. Maybe this is why Nash had given me his blanket—because he had felt the same nameless feeling too. I didn't know what to think. I suddenly wished I was back in the Dome, where everything was as it should be and nothing was a surprise. Nothing was different.

Suddenly Nash appeared on the mountain again, heading toward us. His hands were empty and my eyes dropped slightly. No fire tonight. I looked at him again and froze. He was running.

"Laney! Alese! Theodore!" Nash yelled our names as he came closer and the others looked up from their positions on the blankets as well. He closed in on us and stopped, breathless. He put his hands on his knees for a second and then stood up again. His eyes were bright, his face flushed the color of the sun.

Alese stood up, her eyes wide.

"What? What did you find?"

Nash slowed his breathing and looked at Alese. He had the same expression on his face as the morning before we had come above ground for the first time. The morning before we had come into this world.

"You're going to want to see this." He picked up Alese's blanket and handed it to her. Looked up. "You all are." He breathed and passed his eyes over the rest of the eight. His chest was moving quickly. "Pack up your things. We're not staying here tonight."

Theodore stood too, the memory out of his mind now.

"Where are we going?" he said it quietly, his voice full of wonder.

Nash looked at him, his eyes sparkling.

"You'll just have to see for yourself."

The rest of us shoved our blankets back in our backpacks, Arsen with frustration, probably because Nash wouldn't tell us what he saw. Then we followed him, down a few steps and around the side of the mountain, the rocks and dirt unchanging.

We hadn't walked for more than a few minutes when we came across a cliff that jutted out from the mountain sharply, the opposite of our indents in the Dome. Alese rounded the cliff right after Nash and let out a cry. But the cry wasn't filled with worry, or anger, or fear. It was something else. And when I rounded the cliff, I knew why. This is what Nash had seen.

A narrow valley passed in between the two mountains like a river, snaking out as far as the eye could see and angling up, then disappearing behind the mountain we were on. And the valley was filled, thick to its edges, with trees. Trees.

I brought my hand to my mouth, stood there in disbelief. Trees did not grow this fast, would not be this tall, after just thirteen years. No, this valley in between the mountains hadn't been touched. Somehow, it had stayed hidden from the violent people— the people who had destroyed everything in the world before this one. Everything but us, and everything but this.

Alese was trembling, staring out at the valley, her eyes wet with tears. Then she wiped her face and seemed to remember something. She looked up, her brown eyes shining.

"Theodore! This is what I was talking about!"

He tore his eyes from the valley and looked at the girl with long brown hair. Her face was filled with color.

"These are trees!"

Theodore's mouth opened and he looked back at the valley, back at the tall green creatures with leaves stretching to the sky and thick brown trunks rooted in the grass below.

Alese watched his reaction and her mouth curved at the edges. "Come on!" she squealed.

Theodore sprinted through the rock until he was next to her and then they ran, together, down the side of the mountain and into the deep green valley. They threw their hands up in the air as they ran, and when they reached the grass, Alese turned in circles, her shirt rustling around her.

Theodore collapsed on the grass beside her, his cheeks crimson and his eyes the color of the leaves on the trees.

Alese stopped turning and looked up, the six of us still standing by the cliff and looking at the valley spread out below, watching them. I looked back at her and blinked. I wasn't seeing right. I couldn't be.

Alese's face was glowing, her hair blowing gently in the wind that had turned to just a breeze inside the valley. Her eyes were a brilliant brown, the cloud all but gone from their surface. And then her mouth curved, gently at first but then it filled her cheeks, her whole face. Like something had finally broken inside of her, something that had been there for the past thirteen years, and the five years before that.

She was smiling.

Then she collapsed in a heap on the grass next to Theodore and stared up into the trees.

19

We slept under the trees that night with a fire that lit the sky in yellows and oranges.

After the rest of us walked down to the valley, Alese had picked a handful of bright green leaves and put them tenderly in her backpack. We all found ourselves staring at her, the color on her face and the sparkle in her eyes, confused and intrigued at once.

Arsen looked away almost immediately; it was too much, like the colors were. Even the sunglasses didn't make her eyes or her smile fade. Alese knew that, but it never left her face. It was exhilarating, invigorating, she said. Before, she didn't even know how to smile. Now, she couldn't think of a reason not to. We didn't understand. An image of the boy from my dream flashed into my mind; a smile spread across his cheeks, and yet he was locked up. Locked next to the man with black eyes.

While I lay on the blanket, the crackling heat warming the air, I heard the chattering of some animal up above us. I fell asleep wondering if the world was as surprised by us as we were by it.

The next morning smoke from the charred wood rose in the heavy air, twirled through the trees and up into the clouds. We buried the ashes and set off deeper into the valley. We would still reach the top of the mountain, it just might take a little longer. But to Alese, and Theodore, and even me, it was worth it.

While we walked, Alese brushed her hands across the tree trunks and ran her fingers through the leaves, still in disbelief maybe. She wanted to make sure they were really here, not just a figment of her imagination. Of her memories.

We stopped for a water break when the sun was shining through the branches and creating patterns of light on the grass beneath. Nash looked at me, then at Alese, at the sheer color of her eyes, and back at me again.

Gavin sat on a tree stump and retrieved his knife out of his backpack, then tossed the black bag on the ground. He ran a small, pointed rock across the side of it. Nash looked at him.

"What? I was voted into this group for being able to hold my own. I might as well not damage that reputation."

Nash's mouth creased at the corners and he turned, opened his backpack, and took out his knife. He stood and walked a few steps forward, then stopped. The knife was clenched in his hand, his fingers firm. Then he threw it, with a force that could have killed the boy with the brooding eyes. It landed just a few feet from Gavin, at the center of a tree trunk.

Gavin was staring at the tree, his eyes wide. Then they narrowed and he looked at Nash, stood.

"So softie's got some moves. All right."

Softie? Maybe he had seen Nash give me the blanket.

Gavin walked over to Nash's side and stopped next to him. He looked at Nash, then at a tree a few feet farther away than the one Nash's knife was sticking out of.

"That tree."

Then Gavin threw the knife and it hit the tree he had pointed at, hard.

Dalia and Mallory had stopped drinking water, Alese and Theodore weren't looking at the trees anymore. We were all watching now.

Nash put his hands up in mock surrender and walked to the tree, pulled his knife out from the trunk. Then he retrieved Gavin's.

"Okay, your reputation still holds."

He held out the knife and Gavin looked at him for a moment, then took it. Nash looked down at his knife, then at a tree about a hundred feet before him.

"But it might not after this."

He threw the knife and it cut through the air, hit the wood with a sickening thud.

Gavin didn't miss a beat. He thrust his knife at the same tree and it hit the handle of Nash's knife, bounced off it and to the left, in some bushes.

Nash's mouth curved slightly.

"Next time."

Gavin followed the path of his knife through the trees, scowling. But there was something else there now. A look of respect, maybe.

He disappeared behind the bushes, searching for the blade. Nash went to retrieve his then headed back. He was putting his knife back in his pack when Gavin suddenly returned, his knife in his hand. His face was white.

Nash looked at the knife, then at him.

"Gavin?"

Gavin said nothing. He raised his arm slowly and pointed through the trees, toward the bushes he had just come from. Past the bushes.

Nash's eyes followed. He flicked his knife out of his backpack again and headed to the bushes, Arsen trailing behind him with his knife held out before him. Gavin was behind Arsen.

The rest of us followed, all of us holding our knives in our hands except Theodore.

When Nash rounded the bush, he pushed through tree branches and then jumped back, his finger over his lips and his eyes wide. His face drained of its color too. He motioned for us to stay low. Then he crept forward into the trees.

The moment I pushed the tree branches away I saw a wall. It was made of wood—old, decaying wood, but it was standing almost as tall as the trees surrounding. I looked around, confused. What was a wall doing out here in the trees?

I saw Nash step up onto the wall, on wood that was angled out farther than the rest, and look into an opening. My heart stopped. I felt like I had when my body first hit the water a few days earlier—cold, terrified, my breath nowhere near my lungs.

The opening Nash was looking into was a window. The wooden planks stacked before me were not just a wall. It was a house.

20

I sucked in my breath and stepped back, almost bumped into Mallory. Thoughts flooded my mind. Why was there a house here? How was it still standing? Unless... I swallowed, my throat suddenly dry. Unless people still lived here. The people with black eyes.

I hadn't moved. Mallory looked at me, annoyance passed over her face. She hadn't seen it yet.

If we were a people who touched, she would have pushed me. But since we weren't, she just stood there. Waited until I could feel my legs again. Until I had the strength to move.

I started walking again, slowly. Without breathing, I held my hand out. It was shaking. I placed it on the wall next to me, the wood smooth between my fingers. Everyone behind me had seen it now. We were all beside the wall.

Nash jumped down from the window and waved his arms, motioned for us to go back. I couldn't read his eyes.

When we were all standing in the small clearing where we had just come from, everyone seemed to let out a breath. Mallory's eyes were wild, unbelieving. Alese was pacing, her hands folded on top of her head. Theodore was staring at the trees where we had been. Where the house was.

"Okay." Nash's voice was quiet, nervous. His eyes were fixed on the trees, then on all of us. "Gavin, Arsen, and I will go around back, go inside. Check it out. Theodore, you coming too?"

Theodore looked at Nash and Gavin, then at Alese. At me.

"I'm going to stay. Protect the girls."

Nash nodded.

"Let's go."

Dalia stepped forward, blocking their path.

"Wait. Why do you have to go inside? Why can't we just go around it? We might be walking into a death trap."

She was thinking what I was thinking. That the people with lifeless eyes might still be living. Not just living, but living *here.*

"I agree with Dalia," Mallory spoke. "Let's take a vote."

Nash stopped, looked at her.

"A vote doesn't matter here." He clenched his knife, looked back at the bushes. "If they're still living, the world isn't safe."

Then he stepped around her, Gavin and Arsen looking at her as they passed. They disappeared behind the bushes, behind the branches, and the world was silent again.

The wind passed through the leaves and they shivered, still clinging to the branches. The silence in this world wasn't like the silence in the Dome. Here, there was always something. Always a sound.

Dalia wrung her hands together and stared back at the trees where the guys had just gone. She let out a breath of frustration and sat down on a rock. Mallory was pacing back and forth, her red hair bobbing in its bun. Alese just sat, crossed her hands over her lap and waited. Theodore sat next to her. There was worry in both of their eyes. And in Alese's? Concern. I wondered what it felt like, and then I remembered Theodore. Feeling bad for bringing up the memory with his mother. Was that concern?

Minutes passed, and we waited. I kept looking at the trees, kept watching to see Nash step through. To see them return. The bush shook once and we jumped. I stood. A squirrel scampered past, looked at us, and then hurried up a tree.

Mallory watched with scorn.

"I still think those things are ugly."

Alese smiled a little, amused, and watched the squirrel disappear into the branches. Mallory and Dalia had seen their first squirrel yesterday and they had been as frightened as they were when they first saw the bird. Theodore was calmer. It seemed like he was starting to get used to the things in this world—to expect them even.

Dalia stood and tightened her blond bun, looked out at the trees, then looked at all of us.

"Well, I'm not going to just sit here and wait. If the guys get killed, we're next. I'd rather have a hand in my fate."

Then she turned, her knife in her hand, and started toward the bushes. Toward the wall.

"Dalia, wait!" Alese stood.

Dalia didn't look back, didn't stop walking.

"You can come if you want!" she called out to us, her head still facing forward.

Alese let out a breath, looked at us, then ran after Dalia, her backpack in her hand.

Mallory shrugged.

"Their lives."

I looked at Theodore and stood, ran after the girls in the trees. He followed quickly behind me.

When I pushed through the branches and came to the wall, I saw no one. I stopped and walked slowly along the wood, my hands brushing the surface. My breathing was short, but I kept it as quiet as I could. I couldn't let anyone hear me.

When I had walked a few feet, the wall stopped, and I looked back at Theodore. His eyes were round, but he nodded. I bent down and slowly looked past the wall, around the corner. I saw more wooden logs, another wall. I looked beside it. No one. I motioned to Theodore and we rounded the corner, sticking close to the new wall as we walked.

When I looked around the next corner, I saw Alese and Dalia. They had stopped. Dalia was standing on a rock, staring into another window. She stepped down and her eyes were wide, frantic.

"I don't see them," she whispered it, her voice just barely above the wind. "I should have at least seen one of them walk past by now. They're not there. They're not anywhere."

She put her hands over her mouth. I could tell she was regretting coming over and not waiting like we were supposed to. She didn't know what to do now.

Alese looked back at the window, her eyes wide. She wasn't smiling anymore.

"What did it look like? What's in there?" the words rushed out of me. I hadn't seen a house in thirteen years.

Dalia opened her mouth to speak, to share what she had seen, to tell what was in the house in the trees that should have been destroyed thirteen years ago along with every other house but somehow wasn't.

Right when the first word came out of her mouth, a bush next to us exploded to life, green and brown thistles spraying the air.

Dalia screamed. I fell back against the wall, my knife clamped in my hand, bracing for whatever just jumped from the bush. *Whoever* just jumped from the bush. Then I heard Dalia's voice.

"Arsen!"

Relief flooded my bones and I wiped my forehead, lowered my knife. My hands were trembling.

The tall boy in sunglasses looked at all of us, his face gleaming, his mouth twisted into a sickening curve.

"Come on. There's no one inside."

I put my hand on the wall, steadied myself. Then I followed the others around more walls and to the front of the house. My heart was still beating and I shuddered. For some reason, I couldn't get the look on Arsen's face out of my mind.

21

When we rounded the last corner, I saw Nash and Gavin standing in front of the house with Mallory. Nash's eyes were wide, his eyebrows arched in thought.

As Arsen and Dalia headed to join the others, I took a few steps back and stopped. From here, I could see the house for the first time.

I was standing in a small clearing, one that narrowed and led to the front steps. There was less grass, less nature in the clearing, maybe what used to be a path. Trees surrounded the house on all sides, hugging the walls and making it almost impossible to see by any people who might pass by. It was wood, so it blended in with the thick trunks that were pressed up against it.

The house was old, but it still stood. Its four walls pushed against each other and sagged a little at the edges. The roof was a square of tree trunks pressed together, like the rest. The clearing opened to the two front steps, cracked and in pieces, which were supposed to lead to a small plank that looked like it had once been a front porch. The door was intact, though the glass window that was molded into the frame had been shattered. The house was small, but not too small. A mother and her child could have easily lived here. But if the house wasn't destroyed, where were they?

"Laney!"

Nash motioned toward me, called me over to the group. I swallowed and went to stand with the rest of the eight.

"I think we should spend the night here, wait to see if anyone returns." Nash was talking to them. "It looks old, abandoned. But we need to know if there are others still alive in this world. And this would be the best place to find out."

"You're crazy!" Mallory cut in. Her backpack was slung loosely over one shoulder, her knife nowhere to be seen. "You're honestly saying we just wait here in the killers' house and see if they return. See if they're still alive."

"This might not be their house." Nash turned, looked her in the eyes. "What if it's others? People like us?"

Mallory humphed, put her hand on her hip.

"Well, I don't want to take that chance."

Theodore looked up, looked at Nash.

"I don't even remember houses." His voice was soft, sad. "I wouldn't know what to do with it. Where to sleep or…what to use it for."

Nash's eyes softened. He had forgotten.

"We're only staying here for a night. You don't need to know much."

Theodore looked down, his eyes even sadder.

"Well, I agree with the redhead," Arsen spoke, flipped his knife in his hand. "Not all of us can stay inside. We need someone to keep a lookout, camp nearby. I don't want to sleep in that dump anyway."

I looked at Arsen. Couldn't believe he had called one of the last houses standing a dump.

Nash narrowed his eyes at the word too.

"Fine. You stay out here. Whoever wants to can stay out here. But I'm going in."

Nash swung the door open and walked inside. It bounced a few times on the frame and then closed.

Arsen walked away, past some trees, searching for a place to set up camp. Mallory looked at us once and then followed him.

I looked at the house again, at the front door. Our front door had once had a window that looked just like it. Front steps leading up to a porch too. It was surreal—almost like I was walking through memories. This was a house. I hadn't seen a house in thirteen years, since I lived in one with my mother. The reality hit me suddenly, deep in the chest.

I looked across the group, at Gavin. His eyes were round, lost in memory. He once had a house too. We all did. I wondered if he, Dalia, and Alese felt the same way. I knew Alese remembered. I didn't know about the rest.

"I don't know about you guys, but I'm tired of sleeping out in the open. Bugs and animals everywhere," Dalia said. She took a breath before she opened the door and walked inside.

I looked at Alese, Gavin, and Theodore. They looked back at me, silent.

"Mr. Dabir said we should bring back proof of what love is—proof that it still exists," I spoke softly, tried to still my trembling fingers. Gavin looked up at me. I took a breath. "I'm sure there are things inside that are better than anything we can find out here. Maybe love—" I stopped, tried to believe the words that were coming from my mouth. "Maybe what still exists of love is in there."

Alese, lost in thought, suddenly snapped her eyes back, stood up straighter.

"Laney's right." She wrapped her hand around her hair, looked at Theodore. "We need to do this. For the others in the Dome."

Gavin was still silent, but he slowly nodded.

I didn't know why we were all so scared when we had once lived in something like this. Once lived in this world. But a world is one thing—bodies of water that you once passed by or mountains that you climbed. A house—where living, breathing people made their home, set up their lives—was something else. More personal. It forced us to remember—forced us to think about the destruction, the people who had burned our homes and changed our lives forever.

I put my hand on the doorknob and turned it, pulled. The door opened with a creak. I swung it open wider, took a breath, then stepped into the untouched house in the middle of the woods. I couldn't help feeling like I had the day we all stepped past the thick door, past the bright light. Like I was stepping into another world once again.

22

I blinked as my eyes adjusted to the light. It was darker in here; the windows were small, caked over with years of grime and dirt.

I stood unmoving, looked down at my feet and saw a rug. Red, with a black design twisted into the fabric. It was dirty, stained, unraveled at the edges with large sections missing from the center. I brought my eyes up slowly and steadied myself against the wall. Then I sucked in my breath. It looked almost…livable.

Pictures hung on the far wall, dusted over but the images in the frames still visible. Water with the sun hanging low behind it. Trees covered with something white. There was a couch beneath the crooked pictures, the cushions frayed and slumped in. Next to the couch was a small table made of wood, the same wood as the house was built from. A larger table stood to the left of the couch, in a section that looked like it was once a kitchen. It was surrounded by four wooden chairs. Cabinets were pressed against the wall over a small, round sink. One of the cabinets was open and dishes were still stacked inside, ready for the next meal. Three beds with just the box springs were pushed against the other wall, side by side. The dirty mattresses lay next to them in a heap.

I paused, confused. Three beds? Only two people slept in each household in the world we came from: the mother and her child.

The others had come in behind me now; I had heard the door open and close. They didn't make a sound. I could only guess they were staring at the one room that made up the cabin, like I was.

Small, but with more life than we had seen on our entire journey so far.

I took another step into the house when I realized I hadn't noticed Nash. He was standing behind the couch, staring at another wall that was hidden from sight behind the cabinets. He hadn't moved.

I almost said his name, but the house seemed too quiet, too untouched for such a sound. The floor creaked slightly as I walked over to him and the hidden wall came slowly into view, piece by piece. I stopped. No. It couldn't be.

A large wooden case was pushed against the wall, almost as tall as me. And in that case…I swallowed. Books. There were dozens of books. Some lay scattered across the dusty surface and others were sitting side by side, their thick ends staring back at us. Their colors were faded, but it seemed like all the books were various sizes, which meant they were all different.

I took a step back, looked at Nash.

"These are…" I stopped, breathed.

Nash looked at me for the first time since I had stepped into the cabin. He nodded, barely.

"Books." He looked the shelf up and down, touched one of the ends carefully, like it was made of fire. "I can't believe it."

The others had come up behind us now, their eyes on the shelves in disbelief.

"But how are they here?" Dalia spoke first, broke the silence. "Books were illegal to have in houses. And they were all destroyed. All of them but school books, anyway."

Nash bent down and then stood up slowly, scanning the rows, his eyes passing over the titles on the edges.

"Not here, though. Either someone broke the law, or…" He stopped, looked at all of us.

"Or what?" Dalia's brows were furrowed.

"Or this house was before our time."

No one spoke. I thought I heard someone suck in their breath. Before our time. Before the destruction. Before the world banned love.

Nash turned back to the bookshelf and his eyes stopped on a large, black book with a rounded edge. It was taller than the others, and something was scribbled on the side that I couldn't read. He touched the top of the book and slid it along the surface until it was too far and it fell, landing on the ground with a thud. Theodore jumped. I didn't realize I was holding my breath.

The book landed on its back and its pages were spread open, staring back at us. I stepped forward.

Photographs. They covered the white pages in a faded, dull color that reminded me of the eyes of the people in the Dome. There were four of them, two on each page. Underneath each picture someone had scribbled a sentence or two, a description maybe. But it was what was in the pictures that took my breath away.

The first one showed a thin, blond woman outside, in a garden maybe, clutching the stem of a flower, a large smile stretched across her face. The next one showed her in this very room, years ago, a baby in her bare arms. There were tears in her eyes. The third photograph was more faded than the rest, but there were two people in the small square. The same woman, and a man with brown hair and soft eyes. They were standing on the porch and he was leaning over the railing, his mouth open wide and his eyes full of laughter. The woman was sitting on the steps, her hand stretched out, pointing to the house behind her like she was showing it to whoever was taking the picture. Showing it to the world.

I took a breath. In the fourth picture, the woman was in a long, white dress that stretched behind her as she stood, facing the man, in the trees. He was staring back at her, his eyes deep and his expression something I couldn't name. Something I had never seen before. Never felt. Their hands reached across, to each other, and were clasped tightly at the fingers.

I blinked, confused. This man hadn't left, as other men did before the baby was born. He hadn't left, and he and the woman were touching. They were holding hands. Just like Nash had done with me.

I looked at Nash before I knew what I was doing. He was staring at the same picture, trying to understand it.

Alese stepped forward, ran her finger gently over the page. "They're touching."

She said it like she was shocked and relieved at once. Terrified, and elated.

"That's probably why they're not here anymore."

Dalia said it simply, matter-of-fact.

Nash flipped a page.

There they were again, in photographs spread across the surface. But this time, the man and woman were older. In one of the photos they held not one, but two children in their arms.

Dalia's eyes widened. Alese looked down at the words that were scribbled beneath and read them out loud.

"The Parsons."

Nash rocked back on his heels, thinking. Theodore spoke for the first time since he had stepped through the door.

"Maybe that's the name of the house."

Nash shook his head, still thinking. His mind was deep in some memory he had, something he had forgotten or kept buried, something he was trying desperately to bring to the surface.

"I think that's what they call themselves."

Theodore looked at him, confused.

Alese turned the book slowly and looked at the edge. The scribbled red letters were now legible. She opened her mouth, the words passed over her lips.

"The Parson Family Album."

Silence filled the room. Then Theodore spoke, a whisper that just barely reached our ears.

"What's a family?"

Nash was still staring at the words, his eyes lost in thought.

"I don't know, Theodore." He shook his head, but his eyes never left the words. "I don't know."

23

We searched the house for an hour, for things that might have fallen in the cracks or were simply hidden in plain sight.

When the possibility surfaced that this house was from before our time, before the ban on love existed, everything changed. This house was not just a place to stay anymore, a place to wait and see if humans like us were still alive. It was a step back into history and a look into the lives past. It was a window into how the people before our time lived, and how they survived. How they loved.

The thought baffled me, overwhelmed me. Here, in the middle of the trees, we might have found the purpose and meaning of the word *love*. This is what Mr. Dabir was talking about. This is what would give the people hope and courage to go above ground and once again start humanity.

Alese and I were looking through the cupboards and I ran the tips of my fingers over every intricately designed dish and cup. They were cold, dirty, but not rusty. Only a few of them had cracked or chipped. It was amazing how so many things in this house had survived. The trees must have shielded it from everything.

Dalia had taken on the living room and was searching through the couch cushions, under the rug on the floor. Theodore was outside on the porch, looking underneath the floorboards for anything that might have blown outside or fallen. Gavin and Nash were by the bookshelf, dusting off books and cleaning them until they were legible for us all, setting what looked like important books to the side and leaving the unimportant ones on the shelf. The only unimportant books, we had all agreed before we split up into separate rooms, were books similar to the ones we used for studies.

I was stacking white plates with blue edges back into one of the cupboards when I heard Nash speak.

"Is this even a book?"

I stopped, looked around the corner. Nash was holding a small green rectangle, about half the size of his hand. He had pulled it from behind some larger books that were stacked on the second shelf.

"Let me see."

Gavin held his hand out and Nash handed it to him. Ever since we had come across the books, Gavin had shown more interest in this world and the world before. His dark eyes had brightened a little.

He flipped the thin cover over and opened to a page in the middle. The words were small; I could tell by the way he squinted his eyes.

"Why did the chicken cross the road?" He looked at Nash. "This must be some kind of trivia book."

Nash nodded, interested now.

"What's a chicken?"

Gavin shrugged. Then he spoke, loudly, so we could hear.

"Does anyone know what a chicken is?"

Alese stopped setting cups out onto the countertop and looked at them.

"Chickens? We used to have some!" Her face lit up at the memory. "They're farm animals. They live in a barn."

Gavin looked at Nash and he looked back, his face blank. Gavin didn't know what the small, feathery animals were because he didn't remember anything except the destruction. Nash didn't know because he had lived in the mountains. We only knew what was around us, nothing more—I hadn't thought about how small each of our worlds really were before this.

"Read the answer." Nash nodded to the book, still curious, even though he had never heard of a chicken. My mouth curved slightly. Typical.

Gavin looked down at the page, ran his fingers over the words.

"To get to the other side."

He paused. Looked again to make sure he had read the right sentence.

"Why is a chicken even crossing a street? Shouldn't it be in the barn?" Nash was looking at Gavin, at the page.

Gavin shook his head.

"These people make no sense."

He closed the small bundle of pages and put it on top of the unimportant pile.

The door opened with a creak and Theodore stepped into the house. He was holding something in his hands.

"Guys. Look what I found out there."

His eyes were wide, surprise spread across his face.

Alese and I stopped, and I stepped down from the countertop. Nash, Dalia, and Gavin stopped too.

"It was under some leaves under the porch, halfway buried in the dirt," Theodore was talking quickly, his cheeks flushed. "I thought it was a rock at first. I almost left it there, almost didn't dig it out."

He put the thing he was holding on the wood table next to the couch.

It was small, about the size of two hands cupped together. Some sort of black felt was wrapped around it, but the glue was coming loose, revealing a smooth wooden base beneath. The top was rounded, the bottom a stubby square, chipped at the edges. A small clasp was pressed tightly to the front, directly over a small crack running around the entire piece.

Everyone was next to the table now, staring at the strangely shaped box. I had never seen anything like it.

Theodore was looking at it too. Then he reached over again, touched the top with one hand and the bottom with another. He breathed softly, nervously.

"And then I opened it."

Theodore pulled the box at both ends and it snapped open. Alese gasped.

Inside were two tiny figures, one a girl and one a boy. The girl was dressed in pink clothes that hugged her body at the top and then fanned out once it reached her knees. Some kind of dress. The boy was in black pants and a black shirt that stretched the length of his tiny frame, brown hair dusted onto the top of his head. The figure was attached to a golden metal rod that turned it around in circles—the tiny girl and boy were spinning.

But there was more. When Theodore opened the tiny black box, a sound filled the air. At first I looked around the room quickly, for someone or something that had come in without our knowledge. But it wasn't coming from behind me, it was coming from in front of me. From the box. I breathed in.

The box was *singing*.

There were no words to the song, like there had been when Theodore sang at Collaboration. It was just a noise. A tinkling, ringing, breathtaking noise.

As the sound rose in the air, the tiny figurines circled it, reached for it, chased it. They looked like Alese when she had first seen the trees, twirling through the air like the world had just revealed itself. The figurines didn't have faces painted onto their small heads, but if they did, I was sure they would be tiny, plastic smiles.

Theodore was staring at the box, his eyes round and his face frozen in place. His mind lost in thought—lost in a memory. The only memory he had. Then he started to sing.

His voice reached up and floated with the sound from the box, reached out and touched it, felt it and then blended with it like they were one. One sound, and one song.

Dalia looked up with wide eyes. Gavin and Nash were staring in shock. Alese was looking at Theodore, his parted mouth and his closed eyes. She smiled.

The song was over as quickly as it had started. The figures slowed to a stop and the air became quiet, just a breath against the wind outside.

Theodore's eyes opened and he looked at the box. His eyes were shining—greener than the trembling leaves on the trees.

He reached forward and touched the tiny girl in the pink dress on top of her head, just barely. His hands were shaking.

"I'm sorry," he spoke softly. Tears flooded his eyes and he didn't stop them, didn't wipe them away. "I'm sorry I couldn't stop them from killing you."

Then Theodore broke. His legs shook and he fell to his knees, his hands over his face, tears rushing down his cheeks. He was breathing deep, shaky breaths as he sobbed, his tears dotting the table next to the black box.

I stared, frozen in place, rooted to the ground. I had never seen someone cry like this. When we fell down, or broke an arm as a child, we were allowed to cry for a moment. I had never seen someone cry for someone other than themselves. For another person.

But Theodore was crying for another person. He was crying for his mother.

24

That night we made a fire outside the house, put piles of books next to us on our blankets, and took turns reading pages to each other for hours.

Most of the books were fiction—books about made-up worlds with realistic characters that lived and breathed, went on adventures, and took on challenges, just like us. Then there were the stories that took place in a world just like this one, where men and women sought after, fought for, and even killed, all in the name of love. We guessed these were the love stories, banned from the world when we banned love itself. And with every page that was turned, every word that was read, we could see why they had banned it. Love was a powerful thing that caused some to do whatever it took to have it in their grasp. But maybe this is why our people were so desperately searching for it—it gave you a purpose, something to chase after with everything you have. Something to live for.

All of the books were damaged in some way—water had soaked the words or entire sections were missing. But they were still fascinating. They were bits and pieces of the world that everyone was trying to remember, the world that everyone was trying to make our world like again. The world when love existed, and people existed too. And here they were, clutched in our fingertips.

My hands were white, my breath short. This was more proof of love than we ever hoped we could find.

"Laney, you're next."

I looked up from my thoughts and saw Dalia. She had just finished reading a few pages of a book called *Pride and Prejudice*.

I picked up the book from my lap, opened it. It was a love story, though a little different from the rest. Still, it wrapped around my mind and made me feel like I was there, under the sun, in the cool mountain air.

"I live in a world where love exists. It is more than a vision, a memory, because pieces of it live and breathe in my heart and my mind. In this world love is a tangible object, a thing of the past and the future that causes healing, hope, and lasting relationships that lead to restored people. It is the thing that causes so many to fulfill their purposes in life because with the love they have—the tender hand of a sweetheart to hold or a kiss to dry their dirty tears—all is overcome."

I paused, looked at the words. The rest of the eight were sitting in silence, staring at me. At the book.

I imagined all of us living in a life like this, one with a people who were so sure of this love that they related it to things like hope, healing, restoration, and overcoming. Not just overcoming, but overcoming all.

"Laney?"

I shut the book and looked at Alese, suddenly desperate to discover a life where eyes were not clouded over and people were not still, silent, and emotionless. A world like the one in my book.

"Alese," I spoke and she turned, her eyes glistening in the orange light of the fire. "Teach me how to smile."

Alese's eyes widened, and Dalia's mouth parted. Arsen, who had joined us at the fire along with Mallory, rolled his eyes.

Nash shifted, broke the silence.

"Yeah. Laney's right. We can read all these books, but nothing actually changes if we…" He paused, scratched his head. "If we don't do the things we read. The things that the people who knew how to love do."

Alese's eyes were still glistening and the corners of her mouth curved. She looked at Nash, and then at me.

"You just open your mouth, let it fill your cheeks." She talked softly and touched her cheeks while she spoke. "You can feel it filling your face."

I looked at Nash, and he took a deep breath. Then he did just that. He opened his mouth. It widened slowly, and then faster. When he stopped, his cheeks were pushed out as far as they could go, his teeth opened wide, too wide, I thought.

A laugh burst from Alese's lips. It was the first time she had laughed, the first time any of us had laughed, and yet she didn't even seem to notice. It was becoming natural for her. And it was nothing like the laugh of the men who killed my mother.

"You have to think about something—something that makes you happy. I think that's why people smiled." She ran her fingers through her hair, lost in thought. "Because they were happy."

Happy. We had just read the word in a book and had heard stories from the gray-haired people in the Dome about happiness, but we never really knew what it was. Never really experienced it ourselves. Alese seemed to have found it again—found it in the trees.

I closed my eyes. Happy. I used to play out in the wildflowers every day, even though my mother told me not to. Was that happy? I thought of the Dome, about Mr. Dabir always giving me good grades in my studies, about the day he told us we had a chance to go above ground. I thought about the few months of memories I had before the destruction took over our time. There was a day when I had found a baby bird in the field while I was looking up at the sky. It was next to a large, yellow-orange flower and an overturned pocket of twigs—a nest. I had picked the tiny bird up in my hands and then ran up the stairs, into the house. My mother had been angry, nervous. We weren't supposed to have any animals with us. But then she saw the bird, and her face softened. We nursed the bird back to health, together, for a month. And the day we set it on the green grass and it wobbled, paused, and then leapt into the sky, disappeared into the clouds, was a day I will never forget. My mother had her hands over her eyes, shielding them from the sun.

But I had looked into the sun and watched the bird until I couldn't see it anymore.

I heard Alese gasp.

I opened my eyes, touched my cheeks. They were spread wide. I could feel my eyes clearing, could feel warmth wash over my body and into my heart. So that's what it was like to smile. My mouth opened even wider, in awe and disbelief. I never wanted to lose this feeling, this warmth. It rushed through me like the air I breathed.

I looked up. Nash was staring at me, his mouth wide open in a smile. It looked natural now, genuine, elated. Theodore's mouth was curved too.

"And this is exactly why I didn't want to sleep in the house," Arsen spoke suddenly, his arms crossed. "I'm going to bed."

He stood up and walked into the trees, to the camp he had set up earlier. Mallory stood and hesitated, looked back at all of us. Her eyes were wide. Then she turned, quickly, and followed.

"Don't listen to them," Alese said, looking gently at us. "They'll come around."

25

Dalia and Gavin were staring at us, their mouths open in shock. They had never seen someone smile before Alese, and now Nash, Theodore, and I had done it too. It must be overwhelming to see, like it had been for me.

Gavin spoke, his words jumbled together.

"Hey, Nash. You know that book we found, with the chicken trivia?"

Nash looked at him, surprised. He nodded.

"I'm starting to think that maybe we were missing something. Maybe there was a meaning to it. All of these books are so…they just have so much."

Nash's face spread into a grin.

"I'll go get it." He jumped up and walked a few steps toward the house, then stopped, turned.

"Laney?" I looked up at him. He held out his flashlight. "Will you hold the light while I look?"

I sat rooted to the ground for a moment. Then I nodded.

"I'll go get some more wood for the fire," Theodore offered as I stood. He headed into the trees.

When I stepped into the house, Nash handed me the flashlight. Then he walked to the back of the house, by the bookshelf.

It was even darker in here at night. The corners cast shadows onto the wooden floors, but the moonlight was bright. It shined through the windows, splashed onto the rug, across the table and into the wall. It shined right onto the black box that Theodore had found, still in its place on the table.

Nash turned from where he was standing by the shelf and saw me looking at it.

"That was really something wasn't it? When Theodore sang?"

He spoke and I turned sharply, was jolted from my memories.

"Yeah." I turned back to the box. It looked almost blue now, the moonlight surrounding it in a creamy hue. "That boy has more kindness in him than every one of us combined."

Kindness. I wasn't even sure what it meant, but I knew that it was good. And I knew that Theodore was good.

Nash was holding the green book in his hands and he set it down on the bookshelf again, walked to the table with the small black box. He took it into his hands, held it in his fingers, then opened it. The tinkling, ringing song filled the room again.

Nash stared at the box for a moment, at the tiny figurines clinging to each other and twirling around the platform no larger than my hand. Then he looked up at me. His eyes were wide, sparkling.

"Let's do it," he whispered the words, and I looked at him, surprised.

"Do what?"

Nash looked at me and grinned. Then he turned back to the box, at the tiny figures.

"That."

I looked at the box, my hands suddenly cold. Then I looked back at Nash. At the box again.

"I don't even know what they're doing."

"Neither do I. But who cares?" Nash put the box down on the table again. "You're the one who said we should start doing what the books were saying."

"This isn't a book."

"It's in the house. That means it's from the time when love existed too."

I stopped, breathed. My hands were shaking.

"Come on, Laney." Nash held out his hand and dipped his head slowly. "There are two of them. I can't do this on my own."

I looked at Nash, at how out of place he looked, bending over with his hand out toward me. I thought of the books, and Alese teaching us to smile, and the way it made me feel.

I let out a breath. Nash was right.

"Okay," I spoke, and Nash looked up at me, smiled. "But I'm not touching you again."

Nash's smile faded a little, but his brown eyes met mine. "All right. I guess I owe you that much."

I walked over to the bookshelf and tore a page from one of the books in the unimportant pile. Then I walked back to Nash. He held his hand out to me again. I took a breath and lifted it up, next to his. I hesitated, almost pulled it back. But then I placed my hand in his, clasped his fingers through the piece of paper.

Nash bent down, tore a piece of fabric from the rug, and put his hand on my back, the fabric in between. I smiled. Then he pulled me, slowly, back and forth, to the music from the box.

I sucked in my breath. My heart was beating quickly. I had never been this close to a guy before—had never been this close to anyone before. I could feel the heat from his hand through the paper, could see the curve of his jawline, the smudge of dirt on his neck.

He suddenly pulled me out into the room and spun me under his arm, as the tiny figurines were doing next to us. I gasped, letting go of the paper with surprise. The white sheet fluttered to the ground and came to a rest next to the table. Nash let go of me and bent down to pick up the paper.

"Wait." The words came out of me before I even knew what I was saying. "It's okay."

Nash stopped, still bent down. He looked up at me. I took a breath and nodded. My heart was thudding now. I didn't know what I was doing, just knew that I needed to do it again.

He stood up slowly, and I could see his chest moving in and out. Then he held out his hand. His bare fingers were bathed in the light from the moon. I closed my eyes and then opened them again, looked at the boy in front of me with dirty blond hair. His face was soft, his brown eyes were looking into mine. They widened a little.

I took his hand and warmth shook my fingers, rushed up to my face. I gasped and Nash let out a breath too. We stood there, unmoving, his fingers in mine. The music slowed, and then stopped, the last note fading with the wind.

"How did you know this wouldn't hurt us?"

I found my voice and the words rushed out of me, breathless.

Nash looked into my eyes, his face close to mine.

"My mother. I was walking with her into the trees a few months before our town was destroyed, and I fell," he spoke softly, looked down. "I was sliding down some rocks, and I couldn't stop. My mother, she—came after me. Held out her hand and told me to grab it, even though it was forbidden. She saved my life." He looked me in the eyes again, his breath on my forehead as he spoke. "That's how I knew that touch wasn't all bad. It helped me. So I knew it wasn't going to hurt you at Collaboration."

I was looking into his eyes. They were soft, warm. They almost looked like the eyes of the man in the photo album, staring into the face of the girl with the white dress.

"You know when Alese told us to think of something happy, that that's how we would know how to smile?" Nash spoke again, his breath short.

I nodded.

"I tried to think of something—of some memory I had that would make me happy, but I couldn't. So I opened my eyes and…" His voice trailed off. His eyes were distant. "And then I saw you. The smile lit up your whole face, it was bigger than Alese's had been when she first saw the trees."

I stood there in the silence. My hand felt frozen in place, clasped to his fingers. I didn't know why he was telling me this; I knew I had smiled.

"Laney." The moonlight hit Nash's eyes and they were soft, serious. "I smiled because I saw you smiling. I smiled, for the first time in my life, because of you."

I sucked in my breath and looked up at Nash, at his eyes. My whole body was tingling, trembling. I could feel his every breath, could smell the damp scent of pine and dirt on his skin.

His chin brushed against my forehead, then his lips. He held them there for a moment, and I felt the warmth of his breath. I moved my head, looked up at him until our eyes were level and his lips were inches from mine. I didn't know what was happening—didn't know what this was. I was terrified. But I knew that it felt more natural than anything in this world had so far.

The boy with hair the color of wildflowers touched his lips to mine, and I was running. I was five again, sprinting, twirling, dancing through a field of bright yellow flowers with my arms in the air, stretched to the blue sky, reaching for the clouds. The wind was in my face, the sun radiating through every part of me, reaching around me and through me, becoming me, becoming my every movement and thought and breath.

And then I heard someone scream.

26

I pulled away from Nash and the bright yellow world vanished.

It had been less than a second, our lips barely touching, but it had felt longer. I blinked, released my hand from his and stepped back. My breath was heavy, my head light. The room was spinning.

Nash ran to the door and pulled it open, peered out into the darkness. A scream pierced the wind and goose bumps rose on my arms. There it was again.

"That sounds like Mallory."

Nash looked at me, his eyes wide, and then sprinted through the door, down the steps, and toward the sound. I stilled myself against the wall, begging my head to clear, and then I followed.

There was no one by the fire. It was burning low, the orange flames curling with a thin black smoke that spread into the sky. I looked into the trees as I ran past. I couldn't see anyone.

"Laney!"

Nash yelled my name and I followed it, around some bushes and past trees, into a small clearing. When I reached the edge of the opening, I stopped.

Mallory was standing off to the side, facing the other way, her hands over her face. She was shaking. Nash, Dalia, Gavin, and Alese were kneeling down in the middle of the clearing, on the grass, bent over something. Alese turned her head when she heard me. A tear was sliding down her face. She moved over so I could see, slid over on the grass just barely. My breath left me.

Theodore.

I panicked, threw myself on the ground next to him. His red hair was plastered to his head, his eyes closed. I froze. A bitter taste filled my mouth. Three large gashes sliced through his gray shirt to his stomach and a red liquid oozed slowly out, staining his clothes. The grass next to him was glistening.

Sweet, innocent Theodore.

"But how?" the words choked out of me, fragments of sentences jumbled together. "How did this happen?"

An image of the men with black eyes flashed through my mind, their mouths twisted into ugly grins.

I clenched my fists together, my breathing short.

"Who did this?"

"Laney." Nash put his hand out, stopping me. He looked at Theodore and I saw his eyes in the moonlight. They were wet.

Tears were running down Alese's cheeks now. Dalia's face was white. Gavin was silent, staring. He was in shock.

"It was one of them."

A voice came from the trees. I stopped, looked up. Arsen.

"I was sitting by me and Mallory's fire, and I heard something. Someone struggling."

He walked forward slowly, his body in the shadow but his sunglass-covered eyes on Theodore.

"I got up, went to check out the sound. And I saw Theodore, lying on the ground, cut up. Then I saw a man. He was standing by the trees, wearing dark clothes, a bloody knife in his hand. He ran."

Arsen stopped, looked out into the trees. His face was gray.

"It was one of them."

I couldn't swallow, couldn't breathe. The men with black eyes. They were still alive.

Nash stood slowly, looked at Arsen.

"We can't be sure it was one of them. Did anyone else see it?"

He looked at Gavin. At Mallory. They said nothing. Mallory lowered her head.

"Maybe it was an animal, it just looked like a person. We should spread out, see if we can find—"

"It was one of them!" the words burst from Arsen's lips. He held something in his hands: a piece of black fabric. "I found this on a tree in the direction that he ran. It's part of his jacket. Tell me if you—if any of you—have a black jacket, or any piece of black clothing on you. Then I'll do what he says."

Arsen nodded in Nash's direction. Nash stared at the cloth in his hand. He didn't say anything. Didn't answer.

Arsen's breathing was heavy, slow. He was satisfied with the silence. He looked at all of us once, then into the trees, in the opposite direction the man with the lifeless eyes had gone.

"We need to go. We need to go now."

Mallory's face was twisted in disbelief, fear. She looked at Arsen once and then ran into the trees, toward their camp, where her backpack was. Arsen followed her. Dalia and Gavin stood and looked at Theodore one last time, then ran toward the house, toward our camp.

"Wait!" I yelled the words, desperate. "We can't just leave him here!"

Nash looked at me, his eyes a deep brown.

"Arsen's right." His voice was soft, troubled. "If those people are still alive, we're not safe here."

My eyes fell on Theodore, on his red hair and rosy cheeks. I felt like breaking, sobbing, like he had done when he brought the black box into the house and played its song. I had never felt like this before, this weight on my chest that sucked my breath from my lungs. Not since my mother. And even then, I hadn't loved her. Hadn't known how to love.

I reached my hand out, my fingers trembling, hovering just inches from his face. Then I placed it on his head, touched his hair. It was cold, damp.

Theodore gasped and shot up, sucking in breath and clutching his stomach. His eyes were large and confused. Terrified.

"Theodore—" I breathed the words, stared at the boy in front of me.

He was alive.

27

"Water!" Alese had been sitting in the grass, staring at the ground, when Theodore moved. She jumped to her feet and ran.

Theodore was breathing short, choppy breaths. He looked around him, at the trees. Then he looked at me.

"Someone touched me."

The words stumbled out of him and he gasped, hugged his stomach again.

I looked at him and my heart clenched.

"Yes, someone did. Someone bad. Shhh. Save your breath, okay?"

Alese came running through the trees and knelt beside him again. She put water to his lips and he sucked it in between breaths.

Dalia and Gavin ran back into the clearing, led by Nash.

"Theodore!" Dalia let out a cry and relief rushed across her cheeks. Gavin stopped, watching him.

"Welcome back, little guy."

Arsen burst through some trees to our left and I jumped. He froze and looked at Theodore.

"He's alive?"

The words rushed out of him and he looked at me, at Nash.

"We can't just stay here. You know that, right? They could be back any minute."

"So it's 'they' now?" Nash was beside me again.

"You really think there's only one violent man left on this earth, that he's survived here by himself for *thirteen* years?" Arsen spat the words, his eyes darting into the trees. "There have to be more."

Mallory was next to Arsen, her pack on her back.

"He's right, guys." Her face was still white, still impacted from stumbling upon a bleeding Theodore. "We can't take that chance."

"Then we take him with us," I spoke quickly, abruptly. Everyone looked at me.

"I agree with Laney," Nash said the words slowly, and I looked at him in relief. He nodded gently toward me, and for a second I remembered his lips on mine. The field of flowers. I breathed in a deep, shaky breath. It had all changed in an instant.

"And how do you suggest we get a bleeding, dying boy down a mountain?" Arsen was still staring at Theodore.

"He's not dying!" I snapped. "We can get him back in time. They can save him."

Gavin stepped forward suddenly.

"The trees."

I looked at him, confused.

"The trees," he repeated. "We could make something. Something to put him on. We could carry him."

Nash looked at Gavin, his eyes brightening. He flipped open the knife in his hand.

"Come on."

He rushed into the trees with Gavin on his heels. Dalia followed.

"He's only going to slow us down." Arsen was still standing, still watching. "We'll all be dead by morning."

"Arsen!" the name surged from Alese's lips. "This boy is hurt. He'll die if we don't help him." Her voice was shaking. "Don't you feel anything?"

Arsen snorted. "I *feel* confused that we're going to carry a lost cause down the mountain. Is that enough feeling for you?"

I swallowed. Something had happened to Arsen. He had broken too.

Alese shook her head, looked down at the boy.

"It's okay," she said, trying to smile. "We're not going to leave you."

Theodore looked at her and his mouth curved. His eyes faded and closed, his chest moving slowly in and out.

Nash and Gavin rushed into the clearing, tree trunks in their arms. They dumped them on the ground next to Theodore. Dalia appeared, holding some sort of string.

"I found this in the house today," she said, breathless. "I thought it might be useful."

"Yes, thank you, Dalia." Nash nodded toward the wood and she set the spool of long white string down next to it.

Nash and Gavin put together pieces of wood while Alese, Dalia, and I tied them together as quickly as we could.

We had never done something together before, never worked as a team. It was everyone for themselves in the Dome. But here, with a life at stake and this new feeling—this new desperate, heart-wrenching feeling—nothing seemed more natural. Before, I would have left without a second thought. Now, I couldn't imagine leaving him here, all alone in the black trees.

"We need more wood." Nash had pushed the last two trunks together. He stood quickly.

"I'll come with you." The words left my lips and I jumped up, followed him past Theodore, past Arsen, who was standing on the edge of the clearing, arms folded on his chest.

Nash found a small tree and started cutting the trunk with his knife. I searched the ground, looking for any branches that had fallen.

"You know, I kind of feel like one of them right now. Destroying trees." Nash's eyes were on the trunk, his face somber.

I looked at him, cutting furiously into the wood.

"The sticks we used for the fire wouldn't be strong enough." I stepped up next to him, supported the bending tree with my hands. "It's for a good cause. It's for Theodore."

Nash stopped sawing and looked at me, his eyes sad. He nodded, then started cutting again.

I looked past the tree. The moonlight pooled on some bushes that stirred in the breeze farther up the slope.

"We were so close," I whispered the words, breathed them.

Nash looked at me, then followed my gaze.

"We were so close to the top of the mountain. Seeing the rest of the world," he said, echoing my thoughts. His eyes clouded over. "But we already know the world isn't safe. We're going to have to tell the others in the Dome." His voice trailed off, as if he had just realized the reality of our situation. The world wasn't safe. We couldn't live out here. Once we returned, the Dome would be our lives again. The lifeless people. The glassy eyes. The cold, colorless Dome.

"We'll show them what we found," I said, suddenly desperate. "Teach them how to smile. How to touch. It will be like the world out here, just in the Dome, right?"

Nash's eyes widened suddenly.

"The books!" He looked at me. "Everyone needs to take some, fit as many as they can in their packs. The books are the proof we'll show them."

Nash was right. I couldn't believe we had almost forgotten them. The books were the window into the other world, the world with love. We could show the others what happiness, what love was, try to teach them all we wanted, but the books were the proof. And proof is what they had wanted. Mr. Dabir had said so.

Nash locked eyes with me, pools of brown, deep and frantic.

"I can do this, Laney. You have to get the books before we go."

I didn't even nod, didn't say anything. I turned and sprinted through the trees, back to the fire. When I pushed through the greenery, the air was darker than usual. I squinted my eyes. The fire was out, long black wisps of smoke climbing into the sky.

Relief hit my chest. The books were still scattered on our blankets. The books Dalia and Gavin had been reading were now in a pile on the grass, their blankets gone, taken when they had run to get their things. But at least they were still there. The man with black eyes—if he was out there—hadn't seen the books yet. Hadn't destroyed them.

I collapsed on my knees and started scooping the books into my backpack. There were about a dozen of them, more than one pack could hold, so I grabbed Theodore's backpack and stuffed the rest of the books inside.

Alese suddenly appeared, her breathing quick.

"We're done! It works—we can carry him."

She grabbed her backpack, stuffed her blanket into it, and did the same with Nash's.

"Nash told me to come get you, told me I'd find you here." She looked up at me, saw me zipping up the last of the books. "Do you need help?"

I shook my head.

"Just take Nash's things to him. I think I can handle the rest."

She nodded, turned.

"Alese!" She looked back at me. I held up a white-and-gray piece of cloth. "Theodore's blanket."

She took the blanket and nodded. Her usually soft brown eyes were large. She was scared.

Alese ran into the trees and I stood, balancing the two backpacks in both of my hands. They were heavy, but they had books in them. I should have expected it.

I scanned the ground, looking for anything I had missed. I froze. *The black box.* It was still in the house. I dropped the packs at my feet, sprinting to the house after I did so. The stairs creaked as I stepped on them, and I let the door shut behind me with a bang.

I stopped, let my eyes adjust. The house was silent, with not even the sound of the trees rustling through the windows. Like the Dome. No, it was nothing like the Dome. I dismissed the thought, pushed it from my mind.

I saw the black box on the table. It was still open, the tiny boy and girl clutching onto each other, lifeless. I took a breath, reached over, and took the box in my hand, closing it gently.

I started to turn when I saw the book with pictures, the album, still lying on the ground next to the bookshelf, open. I walked over to it, thought I should take it too. But something felt wrong, like I was taking the heart of the house in the woods. Like I was taking the story—the last bit of love the house still had. I put my hand on the page and slid a single picture out from the plastic sheet around it. The girl in the white dress stared back at me from the photograph. I stuffed it in my pocket and left the book there, on the ground, open to the world, breathing in the air.

I looked around the house one last time. Her house. Their house. The Parsons. Then I walked through the door, away from the first house I had seen in thirteen years, and into the world of black.

28

Light began to smother the sky as the eight of us walked down the mountain, through the trees, with Theodore.

Two people had to hold onto the bed of branches we had created for him, one on each side, and Nash and Gavin had taken it without hesitation. They were walking quickly, clutching the wood in their hands. Nash had taken one of the backpacks with books in them from me and was carrying it on his back. I held the other backpack. The black box was wrapped up in my blanket and stuffed next to the books.

We were walking a different way down than we had come up, because of the reroute through the valley of trees. There were more crevices, more hidden valleys this way, but the other valleys we came upon had only grass. Still, it was easier to hike down on than rocks.

No one said anything as we walked. Dalia led the way and Nash, Gavin, and Theodore were at the tail. I walked just in front of them, to keep an eye on Theodore. Alese had draped the blanket over him and his eyes were still closed, his chest was still moving in and out slowly. Nash had wrapped his own blanket around Theodore's stomach, the second time he had given his blanket away, I couldn't help thinking. The memory of jumping into the lake crossed my mind, but I let it pass. The blanket was already soaked through. Theodore had lost a lot of blood.

There was a rustling noise to our left, and a bird hopped into the air, flapping its wings. Mallory jumped, searching for the man with black eyes. She hadn't been able to speak, hadn't been able to think, since we left the clearing. Her eyes were always darting, always searching. Fear had overtaken her.

"Let's take a quick water break!" Dalia called from the front. "If we tire ourselves out, we won't reach the pool of water by tonight."

She was looking at Nash and Gavin.

I hesitated, looked at the boy with red hair. But Dalia was right. Without their strength, they wouldn't be able to carry Theodore.

I grabbed the strap to my pack and dropped it on the ground next to me. Now I understood why the teachers in the Dome hadn't brought more books. Carrying so many was almost impossible.

We all sat down in the grass, everyone but Arsen. He was still standing, his eyes narrowed. They were on Theodore.

I locked eyes with Arsen, as much as I could with his sunglasses blocking them, and walked over to Theodore. I held my water to his lips. Nash was watching too.

"Arsen, we've been here for almost a week," Nash said, his eyes unmoving. "Your sunglasses are getting kind of old."

Arsen's still-narrowed eyes turned to Nash.

"I'll wear them if I want to wear them. Why do you care?"

Nash didn't answer. He looked at Theodore, then at me.

His eyes were a brilliant brown in the sun, crystal clear. He and Alese's eyes were the clearest of everyone's. Theirs, and Theodore's. They reminded me of the woman I had seen when I was being taken to the Dome. The woman in the window with the brilliant brown eyes, clearer than day. Dalia and Gavin's eyes were clearer than they had been in the Dome, the thick fog lifting a little more each morning. They were trying to see, wanting to see, and wanting to feel. It was stunning how this world could change the colors of eyes, could make them full of life again.

Mallory's eyes were still as gray and lifeless as they had been in the Dome. I didn't understand it. She had been in this world as long as everyone else. And Arsen's eyes were hidden, had been hidden since we were here. But I knew without a doubt that they were as lifeless as Mallory's.

For a brief moment, I wondered what my eyes looked like.

"We should get going."

Gavin.

I hoisted the pack onto my shoulders and continued down the mountain with the rest. We could see the body of water below, and it was incentive enough.

We came to a narrow trail, and I walked behind Nash and Gavin, pulling the blanket back up to Theodore's chin when it fell. We were walking for less than an hour when Nash stopped abruptly in front of me, forcing Gavin to a halt. He stared for a moment.

"Maybe we should go a different way."

Gavin looked at him, then at the trail that opened in front of him with canyon walls on both sides.

"There is no other way. What's the problem? Do you see something?"

Nash said nothing but turned around and looked at me. His eyes were round. He had seen something that he didn't want me to see.

"What is it?" I looked back at him, tried to see past him.

Gavin was looking forward.

"All I see are yellow things growing from the grass. Yellow, circular things." He looked back at Nash, his eyebrows raised. "They're not dangerous, I hope?"

I swallowed, repeated what Gavin had said in my mind. Yellow, circular things. I froze.

Flowers.

It was a valley of wildflowers.

Nash was watching me, waiting for my reaction.

He had heard me talk about flowers reminding me of my mother's death, had seen me stare at the flower on the mountain like it was one of the men with black eyes. That's why he didn't want me to see.

I didn't move. Didn't breathe. Didn't say a word.

"The others are still walking," Gavin said, looking from me to Nash. "We need to catch up."

He started walking forward and Nash was pulled with him, his hand still clutched to the wood that carried Theodore. And then they were no longer blocking my view.

Gavin had been right. A field of bright yellow flowers stretched before us, down the mountain. They bent and swayed with the grass, adding a wave of color to the browns and greens of the rock.

And then all I saw was my mother. I heard her calling out my name, saw the frantic look in her blue eyes. I saw her sifting through the heads of the flowers, searching for me. But it was too late. It had always been too late. The gunshots sounded in my mind and I gasped. I fell back against the rock and blinked, desperate to clear the image from my mind. The field of wildflowers, just the flowers, was back.

"Laney!" Nash was running back to me, running through the flowers.

My hands started to shake, and it spread to my arms, then my chest. Tears filled my eyes and I tried to blink them away. Tried. But I couldn't. They ran down my face, hot against my cheeks. I was sobbing, shaking, crying harder than I had ever cried. Grief overwhelmed me and I cried even harder. Now I knew how Theodore had felt. Now I understood. I had never felt so overwhelmed. So full of emotion. So helpless.

Nash was next to me now. I looked at him, desperate, my face wet.

"I can't," I choked the words, said them between tears.

His eyes were round, creased with sadness.

He looked out at the rest of the eight. They had stopped in the middle of the field of flowers, waiting for us. His eyes turned to me again.

"Laney, it wasn't the flowers," he spoke softly, gently. The way my mother had spoken to me. "It was the people. The violent people. *They* took your mother's life, not the flowers." He paused, locked eyes with me. "Not you."

The tears had slowed. I looked back at him, at the boy who had come back for me. His eyes were confident. Strong. But there was something else in them when he looked at me. The same thing I had seen back in the house in the woods, when we had touched. Was this love? And yet I still didn't even fully know what the word meant.

Nash held out his hand.

"I'll go through the field with you. We'll go together."

Together. The word hit me in the chest. I had never heard someone say it before. Had never dreamed someone would use it about me. But Nash had said it from the very beginning, hadn't he? Before he held my hand up at Collaboration.

I took a breath and reached out slowly. Then I put my hand into Nash's. The feeling of touch, of warmth, rushed through me, and I tightened my grip so I wouldn't lose my balance. The reaction to touch hadn't faded even a little.

I stood and looked out at the field, at the flowers that had haunted me for so long in my dreams. And yet these same flowers were what I had seen when Nash had touched his lips to mine. There was some good to them. There had to be.

I looked at Nash once more and he smiled. I wanted to smile back, but I couldn't. I was terrified.

Then we walked, his hand in mine, up to the edge of the field of flowers. I paused, took a deep breath, and stepped in.

When the first flower brushed against my side, my breath left me. And when I sucked the air back in, I sucked in the field—the deep, rich aroma of the flowers. I was smelling the petals, the warm summer days when I would sit outside for hours, watching birds twirl in the air and the flowers bob their heads to the sounds of the wind. I was smelling my mother, who had come out in the flowers with me, time and time again, just because.

I was smelling my childhood.

I felt Nash's fingers in mine and turned to him, the boy walking by me in the flowers.

"Thank you," I whispered the words, and they felt strange when they crossed my lips. I had never said them before, to anyone. No one said please or thank you in the Dome, because that was gratitude, and that was something we hadn't been able to feel. But I felt it now, like I felt the flowers against my legs.

He looked back at me, at the girl he hadn't known anything about before we came out here, into this world, and his mouth curved again.

"You're welcome."

I looked around again, at the sea of yellow around me, memories twirling like the petals in the wind. I ran my finger along one of the green stems and the stalk was smooth to my touch. I took a deep breath, and then I plucked a single flower. The people in the Dome needed to see this. It was proof of a living world—proof of a world that wasn't gray anymore.

"Laney!" Alese yelled my name as we neared the group, and I hurried to her side. She was kneeling by Theodore.

"Look." She pointed to him, her eyes glistening. "He's smiling."

Theodore had his arms propped against the bed we had made him from the trees. The blanket was at his waist now, still covering his legs. His arms, his face were bare. But he didn't seem to care. He was staring at the sea of yellow around him, his eyes bright and his face twisted in wonder. Awe. Then he whispered a single word, a word we had not heard until we read the love stories back at the house, and a word none of us had felt pass over our lips. A word we might have used when we had first stepped through those gray doors and into the world.

"*Beautiful.*"

29

We still had an afternoon's walk until we would reach the water. There, we would rest for the night. We were exhausted, and if none of us made it back, Theodore wouldn't make it either.

I was walking in front of Nash and Gavin, my jacket tied around my waist because of the warm summer sun. I had gotten used to the colors of the jackets and backpacks now, the colors of the trees and the sky and the grass and the world. I didn't know how I could go back to a world of gray. I didn't want to think about it.

Mallory was walking in front of me, her eyes on the ground. They would snap up, frantically, darting in and out of the rocks around us whenever we heard a sound. But it was always nothing, an animal or the breeze rustling through the grass. Arsen's man with black eyes was either long gone by now, or he was following us, waiting to kill us all. Still, I wondered why he hadn't killed us already, why he was waiting so long.

"Mallory," I said her name without meaning to, probably because it was in my thoughts. I hadn't realized it, but I felt sorry for her— so terrified of this world, so unable to see the good in it.

Startled, she turned and looked at me. Her red hair was still pulled into a tight bun, her glassy blue eyes round.

"Mallory, it's okay." I searched for words. Looked at her. "We haven't even seen the man again. He's probably long gone by now."

She turned forward, eyes still searching.

"Arsen said there's probably more than one. For all we know, he could be getting his friends right now, and they'll all come back for us," she spoke quickly, her breath short. "They'll all come kill us."

I grabbed the straps on my backpack, pulling it up higher on my back. I could hear the crunching sound on the rocks as we walked. I looked past Mallory at the water below. It was larger than it had been this morning.

"We're a few days' walk from the Dome," I spoke to the back of Mallory's head. "We'll make it."

She shook her red bun back and forth.

"I should have never come, should have never volunteered at Collaboration." She kept walking, kept pushing forward. "I should have known this was a suicide mission. It was all for nothing." Her voice trailed off in the wind.

"It wasn't for nothing." My breathing was calmer now, my voice soft. "We learned how to smile, learned how to touch. Learned that touch isn't bad. We saw colors, animals, trees. We saw *beauty*. And now we know what that word means." I looked up to the sky, at the bright yellow sun. "We saw someone laugh for the first time. We have books now! Books to show our people what love is. We may not fully understand it, may not know it all. But we have *enough*. We have enough to teach them, to change them."

Mallory was silent, still walking.

"Don't you see?" I asked, breathless, excited now. "This world may not be safe, but we now have what we need to change *our* world. The people in the Dome."

"And what makes you think they're going to want to change?" Mallory whipped around, facing me. "What makes you think they're going to want to change anything about our world down there?"

I hesitated, confused. We came to a narrow pass along the cliff and I looked back. Nash and Gavin had stopped with Theodore, Gavin moving to the front of the bed and Nash moving to the back so they could fit through.

Mallory followed my gaze.

"What's it like to have someone who cares about you?" she spoke the words softly, irritably.

I looked at her. I hadn't heard right. I couldn't have.

"I see the way he looks at you. We all do. The way he went back for you in the flowers. You were *holding hands*, Laney. We're not idiots."

A chill began to crawl up my spine. Mallory locked eyes with me, didn't look away.

"That's *forbidden*, Laney. And when our people in the Dome see you and Nash touching, they're not going to like it." She looked out at the body of water, at the sky below us, her eyes suddenly sad. "That law has been in place for seventy-four years. What makes you think they're going to change it because of one week?"

I shook my head, desperate, but confident.

"They'll change it. They wanted us to find love, to bring it back to them. That's what we're doing."

"They wanted us to report back about a safe world," Mallory said. "Finding love was second on the list. So with no world to go to…" She paused. Her eyes glanced at Nash, then back at me. "There's no need for love anymore."

No. She wasn't right. I tried to swallow, but my throat was suddenly dry. Mallory was still looking at me. Her eyes were suddenly wet, and she blinked. She put her hand on her hip and stared out at the world.

"I tried to smile, Laney." Her words were quiet now, matter-of-fact. I looked up at her in surprise. What?

She nodded, took a deep breath.

"Back in the trees, by the house. Arsen left to go get some wood and I found some bushes where he would never see me." Her voice was steady, calm. "I sat there for ten minutes, doing what Alese had said, trying to think of something happy. But I could think of nothing. *Nothing.*" She looked at me. I was at a loss for words. She sniffed.

"That's when I found Theodore, when I was walking back to our campsite. But it doesn't matter." She straightened up again, her eyes strong. "I tried. But I couldn't. I guess love only chooses some."

I took a step back without realizing it. I couldn't believe what she was saying. Couldn't believe she had tried. And this whole time I had thought she was just like Arsen.

I lifted my hand to put on her shoulder, to comfort her. Mallory backed away and her eyes widened.

"Let's just go."

Nash and Gavin were right behind us now. Mallory started walking forward again, to catch the others. I stood there for a moment, then looked back at Nash. He was lifting the blanket to check Theodore's wound. It looked worse than before. Nash wrapped it around Theodore again and then pulled the other blanket back on top of his chest. He saw me watching him and smiled.

"Mallory!" Arsen's voice. I turned quickly and my heart skipped a beat.

Mallory was hanging off the side of the cliff, her hands clutched to a root a few feet below the edge, her face white. She had stumbled, fallen somehow. I saw something scamper up the rocks. A rabbit. It had startled her.

I sprinted forward and dropped to my knees at the edge. The world was hundreds of feet below us.

I reached my hand down, stretched it over the side, but there was still a foot's distance between us. I panicked.

"Nash!"

I called his name, but he was already by my side. He reached his hand down and it was inches from Mallory's. She looked below her and looked back at us. Her fingers were slipping.

"Mallory, grab my hand!"

Nash yelled the words and tried to stretch even farther. She could reach him. She was close enough.

She shook her head frantically, her blue eyes wild with fear.

"Mallory, grab it! You can reach it!"

Nash was panicking now. He didn't take his eyes off her, didn't move his hand.

"I…I can't."

"What do you mean you can't?" Nash was desperate now, confused. "You can reach it!"

Mallory looked at us and her face suddenly became sad. Then her eyes met mine. I wasn't moving. My heart was frozen in my chest.

"Touch is forbidden."

She whispered the words and then let go of the root. I saw her eyes fill with terror once more before they were out of sight and she fell, down, through the air, to the world below.

"Mallory, no!" Nash screamed the words and bent farther over the cliff. I pulled him back, away from the edge. We collapsed on the ridge, in the dirt.

I sat there, unblinking, unmoving. Breathing slowly, in and out. Arsen was standing next to us, staring down at the sky. Then he turned and started walking again, without looking back.

My fingers were shaking. My whole body was shaking. Mallory's blue eyes, desperate and terrified, filled my mind.

In the books, and in the past, people had died for love. She had just died refusing it.

30

We reached the water when the sun was at the edge of the sky, just before it would sink down into the blackness.

No one said anything on the rest of the walk. Nash, Gavin, Arsen, and I were the only ones who had seen. The others had seen nothing; they had been too far ahead, hidden by a few sharp corners in the rock. But none of us wanted to share about it—doing so would relive the memories.

We set our blankets a dozen yards from the water like we had done before. I remembered the feeling of wonder, the tears in Alese's eyes when we had first seen this body of water. It felt like so long ago, but it had been only a few days.

I set the bag of books next to my blanket and then walked to the water, away from the rest of the group. The seven of us now. I shook the memories from my mind.

I reached the edge of the water, took off my shoes, and stepped in. It was cool, and it invigorated my tired feet. I stared down at the blue that was slowly fading to black, like the sky. I couldn't see myself, couldn't see my reflection, tonight. The water was as dark as the air.

I heard someone behind me but I didn't turn. I knew it was Nash. The rest of the group was sitting or lying on their blankets, and Theodore was set up next to them. Arsen was staring at the mountains, his face blank. Alese was next to Theodore, readjusting his blanket or giving him water. Dalia was telling Gavin something and he nodded.

"I'll never forgive myself."

I turned. Nash was sitting on the grass with his feet in the water. He looked up at the mountains.

"It wasn't your fault." I cupped my hands with water and soaked my hair, ran my fingers through it.

I looked at him. His eyes were dark against the sky.

"What was she saying to you? Before she…" His voice trailed off. I swallowed. Nash had seen us talking.

I dipped my fingers in the water and ran them through my hair again. Looked away.

"She said the people in the Dome aren't going to want to change."

Nash's eyes creased in thought.

"Why wouldn't they?"

I paused, looked at him again.

"She didn't think love was for everyone, I guess. She said she tried to smile but she couldn't. And if everyone can't love, then it's not equal. And our people won't vote for things that aren't equal." I swallowed, the realization slowly coming to my mind. "That, and this world isn't safe. She didn't think love would be wanted underground."

"She tried to smile?" Nash stared at me. I nodded.

I watched him piece his thoughts together, take in what I had just said. I decided to leave out the part about her seeing me and Nash touch. He didn't need to know that.

"I don't know if I can live like that again." The words came out of Nash in one breath. He looked at me, looked into my eyes. "No talking, no smiling. No touching." He paused. "No you."

I looked at him and he was already looking into my eyes. A breeze swept over the water, ruffling his hair. I looked down, suddenly at a loss for words. He felt the same way I did. The danger of one man suddenly seemed small compared to the size of the world.

I looked past Nash, at everyone else. At Theodore.

"We have to go back." I spoke the words, but I didn't want to say them. "For Theodore."

Nash was silent and looked away. But he nodded.

"I know."

He looked at the water, at the darkness.

"We should get some sleep. We have a long way to go tomorrow."

Then he stood, let the water drip from his feet into the grass, and walked over to the rest.

I squeezed my hair and stepped out, letting my damp clothes hang over my skin in the cool breeze for a moment. Then I followed.

Alese looked up when I stepped into our camp.

"How's he doing?" I nodded to Theodore.

She turned over on her side. Worry flashed through her brown eyes.

"He hasn't been awake since this afternoon, in the flowers." She hesitated. "I think he's getting worse."

I looked at him, at his round face and closed eyes, his red hair. *Come on, Theodore. Just a little longer.*

"He'll make it," Gavin spoke from my left. I looked at him. "I see him smile sometimes, while I'm carrying him. Just barely, but it's still a smile. He's hanging on to something."

He looked at Theodore as he said the words. Alese's eyes widened and her mouth curved slightly. Relief. Hope.

I pulled my backpack close to me and unzipped it.

"I forgot to tell you guys what I grabbed from the house."

I stuck my hand in, past the books, and pulled out the thing beneath.

"The black box!" Alese exclaimed.

Nash shook his head in disbelief. His eyes brightened.

"Maybe it will help him."

I nodded and then pulled the box open. The world, silent except for the sound of the grass bending in the wind, filled with sound. Filled with the song from the box.

Alese smiled and lay back. She closed her eyes. Dalia and Gavin did the same. Nash looked at me once more before he settled back on his blanket, his hands behind his head, staring at the tiny specks of light in the sky.

I wrapped my blanket around me and lay down. I could see the tiny boy and girl spinning around the platform as their song was grasped onto and carried by the wind. When my eyes finally closed, I felt like I was one of them—twirling in the sky while the notes surrounded me.

When I woke, the world was still black. The dots of light were still high up in the sky. I sniffed the air.

Something was wrong.

I sat up and orange and yellow filled my eyes. I sucked in my breath. It was across the field. Something was burning.

I jumped to my feet.

"Fire!"

I saw the rest of the group open their eyes, and that was enough. I ran to the pile of yellow and orange. When I got close, I was coughing. It was larger than the fires we had made each night. Much larger.

"What is it?" Nash yelled the words from beside me.

I couldn't see. Didn't know. But it was more than grass, I knew that much. The pile was as tall as my knees.

I knelt on the ground and crawled, got as close as I could go without the smoke blinding me. I opened my eyes, squinted through the fire.

My heart stopped in my chest.

Something white fluttered in the flames and then melted, was devoured in the orange. As the fire burned its edges and started to attack the middle, I could just see it. Could just see what it was made up of: pages, words.

I reached through the flames and tried to grab it, tried to get past the burning heat, but the flames licked even higher and I fell backward.

Nash ran to me and I started to go back in, started screaming.

"Laney!" Nash grabbed my arms, held me back. "It's not worth it, whatever it is."

I gasped, sucked in breath, choked back sobs. But it *was* worth it. Without it, we were back to a gray world with no proof and no chance of change.

"What was it?" Nash was looking at me, concern in his eyes.

I watched the fire eat away at all of them, the flames coiling in the night sky, before I whispered the answer, the words barely passing over my lips.

"The books."

31

There was nothing left of them.

The fire had burned low and created a pile of blackness—thick, dirty blackness. Ashes littered the ground and were caught by the wind, the remains of the books being carried to some other part of the world. Except no one would know they were books now.

I stood from the grass and wiped my eyes as the sun finally began to uncover its face. The rest were sitting or standing around the burned pile, staring at what remained. Staring at nothing.

The grass was silent under my feet as I walked up to the deep red coals, flickering in and out like the lights in the Dome. Something in the pile caught the light of the sun and I stopped. My heart dropped. The black box was at the edge of the ashes, the black velvet pulled away and the sides melted.

I bent and picked it up, blew the ash off the surface. It was still open from when we had played its song last night. The tiny girl and boy were stumps now, the hinges they once turned on all but gone. I looked it—at the good thing it had once been—and thought of Theodore. He probably would have called it beautiful. What was it now?

"We need to get going," Gavin spoke and I turned to him. Dalia was standing next to him with wide eyes. Gavin turned and looked at Theodore, his eyes still closed on the wooden bed.

I turned back to the pile and watched the last of the coals turn from red to black. I placed what was left of the black box in my now nearly empty backpack and zipped it shut.

"We can tell them." Nash was standing next to me now, and his voice was soft, urgent. "We can tell them about the books."

I stared at him for a moment and then nodded. He was right. We had to try. Maybe if we could prove the world wasn't destroyed, they would believe us about the books too. Believe us about love.

"We need to go. Now." Arsen spoke from his place next to the ashes. His voice was firm, emotionless. "The man who burned the books is around here somewhere. And who knows what he'll do next. The only safe place for us is the Dome."

The only safe place for us is the Dome. Ironic, wasn't it?

Arsen looked at the ashes once more through his dark sunglasses and then turned, heading through the field, toward the grassy slope.

Nash's eyes met Gavin's and they headed over to Theodore, hoisting their backpacks on their backs as they did so. I looked at Alese and she tried to smile, but her lips trembled.

"Those might have been the last books on earth." She stood up slowly, her eyes on what remained. "But they're only books, right?"

Her eyes turned back to me and I could tell she was trying to believe it—wanting desperately to believe it.

"Yeah." I tried to smile back. "They're only books." Books that gave us a bigger window into the mystery of love than we had seen in seventy-four years. But I couldn't say it.

I walked over to where we had slept and picked up the edge of my blanket that was still sprawled across the ground. I flicked it into the air and the dirt on top trickled down. Then something else fell out of the folds. The flower. Somehow, it had gotten caught in my blanket when I took it out last night. I breathed a sigh of relief. If it had still been in my backpack, it would have been burned with the rest.

I looked up and saw Arsen stopped, standing still, watching me. When my eyes met his, he held them for a second then started walking again. Nash and Gavin were behind Arsen now, Theodore in their hands, and I placed the flower carefully in my pack. Alese, Dalia, and I started to follow.

I couldn't help but think of what Arsen had said. If the man with black eyes had burned our books while we were sleeping, what else would he do? I found myself furious and terrified all at once.

When we made it to the slope, clouds began to form in the sky above and it made me think of the damp, white cloud that had covered the air when we had come down it. The way we had slid down the mountain without plan or warning. It was one of the first moments I had begun to feel truly alive—one of the first moments I had begun to truly *feel*.

We took a water break when we reached the top of the slope. Theodore was still motionless, and I checked his pulse. It was weak, a faint sound against the wind whipping around the top of the slope. No one was really talking, and I wondered for a brief moment if we should take advantage of speaking to each other before we were back in the Dome. But the thought passed with the wind. There was nothing to say.

We began walking again in silence, down the slope and toward the green valley with rock walls surrounding. The walk seemed shorter than it had been when we made it the first time. There was no new world to see—no new colors to take in and fresh air to breathe. And yet it was the same world, the world we had seen in all its emerald and turquoise splendor. Maybe that's why the people with black eyes, the lifeless people, had destroyed the world—they had forgotten to take the time to remember everything they had once liked about it. They had forgotten to open their eyes to what was right in front of them.

We were halfway down the slope when Theodore started coughing. But it wasn't a normal cough—he was wheezing, groaning, gasping for breath, like his was all but gone.

I sprinted up to Nash and Gavin, Alese on my heels. They stopped and set him down. Gavin's eyes were round.

I looked at Theodore, felt his face with my hand. He was hot. I looked at Alese and her eyes filled with worry. People didn't get sick in the Dome—there was nothing to get sick from when you lived in a box underground, sealed off from the world above. I knew people used to get sick in the world before, but I had only heard stories. I swallowed, panic beginning to take over my mind. I didn't know how to deal with it—didn't know what to do. And I didn't know if the people in the Dome knew what to do either.

Theodore coughed again, his eyes still closed, and tried to suck in air. His face was white.

I knelt there, frozen, staring at him.

"Get him on his side!"

Nash was suddenly next to me and the panic that had seized my limbs was gone for a second. I looked at him and nodded in haste, helping him turn Theodore over.

Theodore gasped and choked onto the grass next to him. My mouth turned dry. Blood. He had choked up blood.

A loud noise split through the air and shook the sky, sending the grass rolling like waves. Gavin grabbed his knife on impulse and I jumped. The air was thick, menacing, and the sky was slowly turning gray, fading to black in front of us. Over the canyon.

Nash stood, staring in the same direction I was. He breathed in sharply.

"A storm."

32

The clouds were moving quickly, gray masses against the turquoise sky. They were slowly approaching and devouring the blue, making the world a dense, irate gray. Just like the men with black eyes had done thirteen years ago.

"What's happening?" Dalia wrapped her jacket around her as the wind became one strong gust.

Nash tore his eyes from the sky above the canyon and looked at her.

"A storm's coming."

"What's a storm?"

Nash looked at me, then Alese. We all knew—we had been through storms before. The bright flashes, the loud sounds, water pouring from the sky. They had terrified me as a child; I had never been outside in one before. But Dalia, Gavin, and Arsen, they had never seen one before—or remembered seeing one. I tried to retrace my memories, but I couldn't remember the clouds ever being so dark.

"Imagine if the world got angry," Nash yelled to Dalia over the sound of the wind. "That's what's about to hit us."

Dalia didn't answer but looked back at the sky.

I saw Arsen out of the corner of my eye. He had one hand over his eyes and the other clung tightly to the strap of his backpack. He looked nervous. Arsen never looked nervous.

"Well, we better get going then." Gavin bent and grasped the side of Theodore's wooden bed. "The Dome's just through the canyon. Once we make it there, we'll be safe."

Nash nodded and picked up the other side of the bed, but his eyes never left the clouds.

We were nearing the bottom of the slope when drops of water started to fall from the sky. Dalia wiped the drops off one by one at first, as if she didn't know where they came from. Then she stopped and looked back at us, her face filled with confusion.

"Where's the water coming from?" she demanded, wiping another drop off her face.

Nash said nothing but nodded up, toward the clouds. Dalia followed his gaze and her mouth opened.

"You've got to be kidding me."

Gavin stopped behind her and wiped his face with his free hand. "What's it called?"

Alese was staring into the sky, her face bright.

"It's called rain."

A bright flash lit up the clouds, followed by another sound that pounded the air. And it was this sound that seemed to open up the sky, to spread the clouds like cotton and let everything that was waiting on top fall through. There was no holding back, and there was no reason to.

"Run!"

I don't know who said the word, but I ran. Nash and Gavin hoisted Theodore's bed to their chests and followed.

The rain came down in sheets, clinging to my skin and drenching my hair and clothes. The air was so heavy, the rain so thick, that I could only see the boots of the person in front of me, leaving footprints in the wet grass that were soon lifted up by the wind.

When we reached the mouth of the canyon, I stopped. Didn't there used to be grass here? The floor inside the towering brown rock was covered with a thin layer of water. It looked like the blue pool we had slept next to. I swallowed, staring at what lay before us. The canyon was flooding.

Arsen was already splashing through the walls of rock, his hands covering his head. The water was up to his shins.

"Laney, we have to move," Nash yelled the words as he and Gavin ran past me. "We might not have much time!"

I took a breath and stepped into the water rushing from the mouth of the canyon. The pull was strong and the force of the water took me back a few inches. I gasped and grabbed the rock next to me. I had never been in water before. The lake, yes, but that was different. Calm. I didn't know what to do.

"Laney! The rock!"

I heard Alese over the wind and saw her pressed against the canyon wall across from me, slowly inching her way to the front. She was holding onto the rock for balance. And it was working.

I grasped onto the rock wall next to me and, hand over hand, began making my way as quickly as I could to the other side of the canyon. Nash and Gavin were in the middle of the canyon, holding tightly to Theodore as they pushed their way through the water. Arsen was almost at the other side. Dalia was clinging to the rock behind Alese.

A bright light lit up the air and the flash filled my eyes for a moment, blinding me. When I opened them, I saw Gavin standing in the middle of the canyon, alone. Nash was behind him, holding tightly to one side of Theodore's bed while the water pulled the other.

Gavin tore his backpack from his shoulders and dove into the water, toward Nash. Nash was holding the bed with both hands now, his face scrunched in pain.

My eyes widened. Gavin's backpack was hurling through the water, tossing and turning, heading straight toward Theodore.

"Nash!"

But he couldn't hear me.

The backpack slammed into the side of Theodore's wooden bed and cracked it in half. Nash's eyes grew large and he grabbed Theodore's hand before the wooden tree trunks scattered and floated down the canyon.

Gavin was by Nash's side now, but Nash yelled something to him and hoisted Theodore's body on his back. Gavin stared at him for a moment, the water running down his face. Then he turned and started pushing toward the end of the canyon again.

I looked at Theodore, at his limp body hanging over Nash's shoulders, and started walking again. Quickly. We needed to get him back.

It seemed like I had been walking for hours, pushing against the rushing wall of blue, when the door of the Dome came into view. Relief rushed through my mind, but with something else. Regret. Memories of a world where gray was the reality, nothing else. I stopped, grasped onto the rock with the rain pouring down on me. Should we really go back?

When I saw Theodore, I pushed the thought from my mind. He needed this. He wouldn't survive out here. And they would change, the people with gray eyes. They would change when they saw that love still existed.

"Let us in! We're back!" I heard Arsen's voice when I got closer. Everyone was next to the large gray door, holding onto the cracks in between the door and the rock. Gavin and Dalia joined him, banging on the upper half of the door. The bottom half was in the water.

"Mr. Dabir, if you don't come up here right now, you'll regret it for the rest of your life!"

Arsen was screaming now, his voice desperate, terrified. Alese looked at him and her eyes widened. She was standing on the other side of Nash, her arms wrapped around her chest.

I was shivering; the water enveloped my legs like a blanket. I couldn't remember ever being this cold before.

The sky flashed again and suddenly I was standing in my bedroom and staring out at the water that was pouring down on our town. I was four. The sky was a deep gray, and I was shivering. Not because I was cold, but because I was afraid. I heard the door open behind me and my mother came in the room, her blue eyes soft. She sat down next to me, and when the room lit up again, I wrapped the blanket tightly around my shoulders.

"Laney, look at the rain." Her voice was gentle, nostalgic.

I looked up at her and her eyes brightened for a brief moment before she nodded toward the window.

"Watch the way it falls onto the rocks and splatters on the porch." She breathed in, and I could see her chest move. "If you look closely enough, you can see pictures on the wood. Pictures that the rain made."

I followed her gaze and looked at the damp brown slab of wood that spread in front of our door. The drops splattered in circles, with other drops staining the surface around it. I sucked in my breath. They almost looked like—flowers.

My eyes widened and I looked at my mother again. Her eyes crinkled at the edges.

"See? Everything has a little good in it." She looked back out at the storm. "No matter what they say. Everything has a little—"

The air boomed and shook the water around me. I blinked. I looked around, squinting through the rain. A memory. One I never knew I had until now.

Gavin had stopped banging on the door, and Arsen's voice was quieter, his fists softer. Alese was staring at the gray slab with sadness in her eyes. Nash held onto Theodore with both hands, his eyes on the door. The hope that he had held onto for so long draining from his eyes.

The rain continued to fall around us, splashing in the water that slowly continued to rise. I closed my eyes, listening to the storm and clinging to the face of my mother.

No one said anything. No one moved. Our eyes were all on the door we had come out of so long ago, or so it felt. Our confidence in a people that only knew gray walls and glassy eyes.

I was grasping the rock when I felt the door move. I stepped back in surprise and looked around at the others. They hadn't moved, their faces hadn't changed. The door shifted again, just barely.

"Someone's here!" I said the words before I could process them.

Arsen looked up, put his hand on the door next to mine. It moved again. Someone was pushing it.

"Everyone grab the door!"

He yelled the words and grasped onto the edge of the gray slab. Gavin, Dalia, and Alese looked up in surprise. They pushed through the water and put their hands on the door. I did the same. The rock felt cold on my fingers.

"When I say three, push!" Arsen shouted the order. He grasped the door tighter.

"One. Two." I pressed my hands against the door and braced myself. "Push!"

The five of us pushed against the gray door with all of our strength. The door crashed open and water began rushing in. The Dome. It would flood if we didn't get in soon. I hadn't even thought about it.

"Hurry!" Gavin yelled the words and I pushed myself toward the opening, the door to the other world. The rain filled my lungs and I fell back, coughed out water, stood again. The door was still open, and I couldn't see anyone else.

I pushed through the water and up to the door when I felt someone take my hand. Warmth rushed through me, and for just a second, I couldn't feel the water anymore. I looked behind me.

Nash.

We stepped through the door together, Theodore on his back, into the world of gray. Into the Dome.

The door slammed behind me, and Nash's hand squeezed mine for a brief second. Then he released it. The warmth vanished, and with water dripping down my face, I found myself wishing I had looked back at the storm one last time.

33

It was everywhere, and nowhere. It filled my eyes like the light had just moments before. Everything was a blur for a moment, a blob of paint that spread out before me in the small room. A blob of gray—cold, ordinary, poignant gray.

The others stood before me, motionless, staring into the emptiness before them. It was the world we had come from so many days ago, and yet it was everything but.

I closed my eyes. Opened them. Closed them again. I remembered the room, but it had seemed normal before. A part of life that would always be with us, and that should be. I remembered silence and hollow air, but not like this. Then, it was just something that was. Now, it seemed like something that shouldn't be. Something that was taunting us, hiding a secret that would never break through the thick walls. Something that was keeping us from another world.

The thought was staggering, and I blinked. The lack of light hurt my eyes.

"Well, well," Mr. Dabir spoke, his voice a blade in the silence. "Look who's back."

We all stared, our clothes dripping on the stone floor. I could hear the drops hit the ground and then spread, covering the floor with a thin layer of water. Just like the canyon. I paused, listening, but I couldn't hear the storm through the door.

"We would have been back even sooner if you had answered the door right away." Arsen was the first to respond and he grumbled, his eyes on the ground.

Mr. Dabir straightened and pretended not to hear what he had said. He adjusted something on his face. Sunglasses.

"I'll call for Collaboration immediately." He ran his eyes across all of us and stopped on Alese, then me.

"I'm going to assume your hair came undone in the storm. I will give you a moment to tie it up again."

I looked at Alese and she hesitated, then reached in her pocket, grasped a string, and tied her long brown hair in a bun. I didn't want to, but I did. Tying it up felt like I was losing something.

Mr. Dabir nodded and then looked at the stairs. "We were readying others, you should know. We thought you weren't coming back." He swept his arm toward the long, cold staircase. "Shall we?"

I clung to the straps of my backpack and looked at Nash. He was still holding tightly to Theodore's arms. Mr. Dabir hadn't even mentioned him.

"Mr. Dabir, Theodore's hurt." I took a step forward, suddenly breathless. "We need to help him."

"Help him?"

Mr. Dabir stopped walking, turned back to me. I realized he had probably never used the word before, much less knew what it meant. He turned to Nash.

"We have no doctors."

My heart dropped.

"I'm sure there's someone in here who knows something about healing." We had come all this way. I wasn't giving up now. "Someone who remembers. We could ask at Collaboration, make an announcement—"

"Any announcements made at Collaboration are for the good of all the people." Mr. Dabir looked at me, his eyes unblinking. "How is healing the boy for the good of us all?"

Nash stepped forward, his fists clenched around Theodore's arms. "You can't be serious."

Gavin moved by his side.

Mr. Dabir didn't flinch, didn't say a word. He just looked at Nash, then at Gavin and Alese, at Dalia, and then me. His eyes widened, barely. He was seeing something for the first time. Our eyes. He knew we had changed, however much we had.

"We will put the boy in the room that we put the others before they died." He paused. "If he survives, he was meant to survive, and he will rejoin us. If he dies, he dies. He is no use to us anymore."

Mr. Dabir paused then slowly lifted a finger, pointed it at Nash.

"And you…" His voice broke off. He looked at Nash's hands. "After you put him in the room, you are never to touch him again. Touch"—he took a breath— "is forbidden."

I swallowed as I listened to his voice. The words were twisting my lungs, squeezing each and every breath. He was talking about the other three. The three that made us ninety-seven instead of one hundred. Mallory had made us ninety-six. Now we would be ninety-five.

"You can't do this," Nash said the words slowly, calmly. "You're killing him. Just like they killed us thirteen years ago."

"*They* had no moral compass!" Mr. Dabir's voice rose and his cheeks reddened. "We have laws. And our laws say what is not done for the good of us all is not done." His breathing slowed. He smoothed his shirt. "We are nothing like them. I am nothing like them."

I looked at Nash, and at Alese, at the tears forming in her eyes. She was shaking her head.

"So are we going to go tell the people what we discovered on our long and treacherous journey outside the Dome, or what?" Arsen looked at Mr. Dabir, the sunglasses still on his eyes.

Mr. Dabir blinked, then seemed to realize why we were there once again.

"Yes, right." He nodded at Arsen, at all of us. "Come. They will be interested in what you have to say."

Mr. Dabir walked toward the stairs again, followed by Arsen. As Arsen passed, he bumped hard into my side. My backpack fell on the ground, scattering its contents across the floor. I knelt down quickly and scooped everything back into the largest pocket. Arsen knelt beside me.

"Oops." He looked at me, his mouth curving into an ugly smile. He stuffed his hands into his pockets, stood, and kept walking. I glared at him. He didn't turn around. Theodore was nothing to him. None of us were.

"I'll figure something out." Nash was next to me, helping me place the last few things in my pack, and he spoke softly. "I'm not leaving him there to die."

"*We're* not leaving him there to die." Alese stepped by us. Dalia and Gavin were by her side. "We're in this together now."

I nodded. Together. For the first time in my life, I felt grateful. Grateful for these people. I swallowed. How I had lived my life for so long without them was overwhelming to think about. I couldn't imagine doing any of this without them now.

Alese put a hand on Theodore's arm and tried to smile.

"It's going to be okay, Theodore."

I watched her in silence, her words repeating in my mind. It was going to be okay. It had to be okay. Once they heard what we had to say, the people down here would want to help.

Gavin and Dalia looked at us once more and then headed for the stairs. Alese reluctantly took her hand from Theodore's arm and followed. I nodded to Nash and we moved our feet forward, step by step, to the stairs, then started the descent that seemed to go on forever. I couldn't help thinking that I had gone down these stairs one too many times. And I had only gone down them twice.

"Isn't it splendid?" Mr. Dabir's voice echoed through the spiraling walls as we descended toward the Dome. "And an old war bunker, to say the least. Every time I descend these stairs I'm taken all over again. I bet you are relieved to be back."

I glanced at Nash. Was he serious? Mr. Dabir was the one who had wanted us to discover the world above and what lay in it. And instead of asking us how it was—what waited in the world our people hadn't seen in thirteen years—he talked about the splendor of the Dome. The Dome. He didn't even know what splendor was.

"They're not like us, Laney." Nash's voice was a whisper behind me. "Remember? We used to think gray was normal, beautiful even, too."

I hesitated, nodded. Nash was right. All of the people down here had no reason to see the Dome as anything less than perfect. It was all they knew. It was all we used to know.

My hands grew cold as we neared the bottom of the stairs and headed to the center of the Dome for Collaboration. This world was gray now, but it was all about to change. A piece had been missing for seventy-four years, and we had found it again. We were about to change everything.

I watched as the others descended deeper and deeper into the Dome. I wiped my hands on my shirt. Collaboration couldn't come soon enough.

34

When we stepped off the stairs and onto the ground floor, Mr. Dabir made us take off our bright jackets and stuff them in our packs. Then he guided us to the room where the others had died. He said he couldn't stand to see Nash touch Theodore any longer.

It was a small, gray room with a bed pushed against the wall, much like the rooms we had all stayed in. When Nash lay the redheaded boy on the bed, Alese covered him with a blanket, and I checked his pulse. It was weak and pressed lightly against the skin only every few seconds. He would be dead soon—he had been unconscious for almost a day, and the bleeding hadn't stopped. Mr. Dabir frowned at me when I touched him, but I pretended not to see.

Then I stepped out, slowly, glancing back every step, and the door was shut with a thud. We were almost down the hall when we heard a sound. I stopped suddenly, turning. Nash stopped too.

"Help! Somebody help me!"

The terrified plea erupted into a fit of coughing.

I froze, and the reality hit me in the chest like the icy water from the storm.

Theodore.

My breath rushed back into me and I sprinted down the hall to the room.

"Laney!"

I didn't turn around.

"Laney. Come here immediately."

I stopped, breathing hard. Mr. Dabir was looking at me with firm eyes.

"But he thinks he's alone," I breathed the words, sucking in the thin air from the Dome and looking frantically at the door.

Mr. Dabir looked at the others, then back at me.

"He is alone."

When we reached the center of the Dome, it was already full of people. I could hear the silence even before I stepped in the room. No one moved. No one even seemed to breathe. This had become their reality. This had been *my* reality, for thirteen years.

Ms. Geena saw us and motioned quickly toward the platform. Arsen was in the front as we all headed toward her. I found myself wishing I could grab Nash's hand—like the day he had first grabbed mine, here, on the podium, in the middle of all the people.

Mr. Dabir was the last to reach the center. He stopped next to Alese.

I paused, closed my eyes, took a deep breath, and turned. Then I opened them.

The people stared back at me, glassy eyes with tight hair and pale skin. Their eyes didn't even blink, lips didn't even part, at the sight of all of us returning from the world above. Well, all of us but one. The sea of lifeless faces before me became a blur. Nothing had changed. Everything was exactly the same.

"The eight have returned." Ms. Geena's voice echoed through the microphone and around the cold stone walls.

Gavin was standing next to her and he cleared his throat. "Seven."

She looked at him, confused.

"Only seven have returned."

Ms. Geena swept her eyes over us and then straightened, as if she had just realized something. "Oh. Well, the seven have returned!"

Her voice rang through the room once again and she smoothed her shirt and looked down at her clipboard, going on with the scheduled event.

I caught Nash's eye and he looked back at me, his eyebrows creased. They hadn't even noticed Mallory and Theodore were gone, and they didn't seem to care. I shuddered, wondering how this had once been me.

"They were the first of us to go into the world above after thirteen years—when it was destroyed. And now they will relay what they saw."

Ms. Geena stretched the microphone toward us in her white fingers.

"The floor is yours."

None of us moved at first. Then I heard a shuffling, someone stepping the few steps to the front of the platform.

Arsen.

I tried to swallow. The realization trickled through me that he shouldn't be going first.

When Arsen took the microphone from Ms. Geena, he said nothing for a moment. Just stared out at the crowd. Then he spoke.

"From the moment we stepped into the world above to the second we walked back into the Dome today, I had one thought running through my mind."

Arsen paused. The silence was painful.

"Why look, when you already have something worth looking for?"

I raised my eyes. Ms. Geena was taking in every word. Arsen had stopped again. Where was he going with this?

"This Dome is everything we need and everything we could want." He swept his eyes from the crowd to Mr. Dabir. "This man even said it—the Dome is splendid! A perfect world for a perfect people."

I shook my head, looked out at the people. Some of them had moved, just slightly. If I had seen right, they had nodded. Arsen went on, and his voice became grave.

"The people with black eyes still live." Ms. Geena's mouth opened slightly. Mr. Dabir seemed unmoved—untouched. The people in the crowd were still watching with blank eyes, as if the words Arsen was speaking were from our books used for studies.

"They hurt Theodore, they killed Mallory, and they will kill all of you." Arsen blinked, and his voice softened. "But it doesn't matter. They can have their world. We have ours."

"But their world is beautiful!" The words rushed from my lips before I could stop them.

Arsen stopped, stiffened. Ms. Geena looked at me, baffled by the word I had just used. Someone in the audience shifted.

"Here—imagine this." The words were coming quickly now. I had to make them see. Could they even still imagine things? "Emerald grass stretched before you in a field. Massive mountains spread out as far as you can see. Water—clear, crystal blue water. A turquoise sky that fades to crimson as it blends into the sun."

The images were rushing from my mouth, the snapshots of the world above coming back like the first time I had seen them.

"Some of you are older—lived for years, decades before the world was destroyed. Don't you remember? Don't you miss it?"

I paused and looked out at the crowd. They were still staring, still glazed over with indifference and disregard. I shook my head, pleaded for them to listen in my thoughts.

"There were trees."

Another voice. Alese stepped forward, her eyes sparkling.

"Tall, brown trunks with bright green leaves." She breathed in. "And wildflowers. Yellow, the color of the sun. They were the most magnificent things you will ever see."

Nash stepped forward and nodded. "The world isn't destroyed anymore." He looked out at the people and I did the same, tried to stare in the eyes of each and every one. "It's breathtaking."

"And we found love." When the word left my lips, the room seemed to come to a halt. All eyes shifted to me. "We learned how to smile, we learned how to laugh." I took a breath and my eyes fell on Nash. "We learned how to *feel*."

Nash looked back at me. I thought of the books and wished, more than anything, that I was holding them in my hands right now.

Mr. Dabir held up his hand and relief spread across Arsen's face.

"And do we have proof of this—intact—world? This love?"

I grabbed the strap of my backpack, flung it off my back and on the platform. The flower. It wasn't the books, but it was something. It was a start.

I reached my hand past the blanket, sifted through what was left of the food. My fingers hit the bottom. The sides. I hadn't seen even a petal of yellow. My heart beat faster, and I searched again. Then again. I knew it was in there. I had placed it in after the books were burned, before we came to the Dome. No one had touched my backpack. No one had—

I froze.

One person had. Arsen.

I looked up and he was watching me. His eyes met mine, and he winked. The same dirty grin he had given when he bumped into me in the room by the door to the world started to spread across his face, but he suppressed it. Then he looked away, back out at the people, his sunglassed-face stone once again. Now that I thought about it, why was he still wearing sunglasses?

"Arsen. Why did you take it?"

I stood and he looked over at me again, surprise flashing across his face.

"Take it? Me?" He looked at the rest of the six, his eyes pausing on each and every one. "It was probably the men with black eyes." A twisted grin tugged at his mouth once again, and this time he couldn't stop it.

The breath rushed out of my lungs and the silence pounded my ears. It couldn't be. Our people weren't like them, would never do bad things. Would never hurt others and destroy books. Arsen would never do something like that.

Would he?

Arsen was the only one who had ever claimed to see the man with black eyes. No one else had. He hated the world, but he needed a reason for everyone else to hate it too. This had been his reason—it had to be. A rush of images filled my mind—his eyes widening when he saw Theodore still alive, his haste at always wanting to leave, when he stared at me while I placed my flower back in my pack, his distaste of the books. This explained why the world wasn't still destroyed—because there had been no one left to destroy it. Not until Arsen crossed through the door.

I froze. A sour taste filled my mouth.

Arsen had stabbed Theodore.

"It was him," I said the words, outrage overwhelming me. "There were never any men with black eyes. He's the reason Theodore is dying!"

In a normal world, a room would have erupted into rage, into disbelief. But no one moved. No one except the people on the platform.

There was a pause, and then Nash and Gavin rushed Arsen and he jumped back, put his hands over his face. Alese stepped next to me and grabbed my arm, looked at me, her brown eyes not wanting to believe it, but slowly widening as everything became clear. Dalia's eyes were narrowing, her arms crossed over her chest.

"Stop!"

The word pounded the room, rang against the walls and made even the glassiest eyes widen for a split second.

Mr. Dabir stood, his face red and his chest moving quickly in and out.

"Blame, violence, disorder—this world you speak of has made our fears come true. It has turned you all for the worse." He paused. His hands trembled for a split second. "It has turned you into *them*."

He spoke the words, and they were like a blade in my heart.

"Lock them up. Lock them up now."

35

We were taken down hallways, past the supply rooms, into a black classroom that led to another hallway, dark, like the rest.

I blinked and my feet stopped moving before I was told to keep walking. It was my dream. The hallways, the screaming.

I breathed in sharply.

A boy with dirty blond hair and striking blue eyes watched us as we passed. He pressed his hands against the glass and his eyes widened.

Lander.

He was real.

"I wish we had more rooms, but this will have to do for now." Mr. Dabir swept his eyes toward the third room in the hallway. "We're still cleaning that one."

I followed his gaze to the other room. The man with black eyes had been in there. He had been down here, with us, for who knows how long. I shuddered, wondering what had happened to him.

"Laney." A sharp voice broke my gaze. Mr. Dabir stared at me. "You too."

"Mr. Dabir, you can't do this," I pleaded. "We found love! We can show you, we can change the people—"

"If what I saw out there on that platform is love, I want nothing to do with it." Mr. Dabir didn't move. "Maybe Arsen is right—we have everything we could ever need."

He looked at me once more and then nodded toward the room. *No.* What they had seen at Collaboration wasn't love. But they didn't know that, did they? My throat went dry. That had been our chance to change it all, to prove that love still existed. What had I done?

I walked into the room in a daze, my chest heavy. This wasn't happening.

I stood next to Alese, Gavin, Nash, and Dalia when a thought filled my mind.

Theodore.

There was no way to help him now, no way to sneak back into the room. A sickening feeling filled my chest. I had killed him.

Mr. Dabir pressed a button and the door slid shut, the lock clicked into place. He looked at us—the five of us—one more time, shaking his head back and forth slowly. Then his glassy eyes turned and he walked back down the hallway and out the door.

No one spoke at first. It was like when we had first met—silence, cold air, and gray walls.

"So you found it?"

A voice broke through the silence, echoed down the hallway. It came from the other room.

The others looked at me, more confused than anything else. They had never seen him before, had never known the Dome kept people locked up, away from everyone else.

"Lander?" I found my voice, and it filled the empty room.

The voice down the hall chuckled. "Who else?"

I nodded to the others, showing that it was okay. That he was okay. I didn't know much about him, but I knew he had the clearest eyes I had ever seen.

"Yes. We found love—or as much as we could find in a few days. At least, I think we did." I was speaking to the wall, to the empty air. I wished I could look into his eyes.

"I could tell." Lander's voice was softer, wistful. "I could see it in your eyes."

Silence filled the room again, and then Dalia straightened. "Who are you? Why are you down here?"

Lander was silent for a moment, but then he spoke again.

"I lived with my family until just a few years ago. Our house was small but perfect—my grandparents, my parents, and my brother, all in one place." He paused, but in my mind I could see a smile spread across his face, then fade. "We didn't even know the rest of the world was destroyed."

Nash's mouth widened.

"You were still out there? You weren't taken down here thirteen years ago like us?"

"No." Lander's voice was sad now. Longing for something—something that wasn't here anymore.

"One day I woke up, and my parents were gone." He took a breath. "I think they found out about the violent men somehow, so they went to see how bad it was. My grandparents and my brother—he was older—went after them, but they never came back. So I went looking for them, and I found this place." His voice shook, but then became still again. "Mr. Dabir—the others that came to the door—locked me in here because they were scared. My eyes—they had never seen clear eyes before." He almost said something more but stopped.

"You actually lived with your—" Alese's eyes widened. "Your mother and father? You had a brother?"

Lander laughed softly. "Yes. My family."

So that's what a family was. A picture of the black album, the word *family* scribbled across the end, filled my mind. I wondered what it was like to have more than just a mother.

"But how—?"

"We lived by ourselves, followed our own laws." Lander's voice broke in gently. "Seventy-four years ago we agreed, as a family, not to ban love with the rest of the world. So we didn't. It's been carried on through the generations—carried on to me."

Silence filled the air again. They hadn't banned love? But that meant—that meant Lander had lived with it all along. Never stopped living with it.

My head felt light, and I pressed my hand against the cold wall for balance. I guess that explained his eyes, as unblemished as the turquoise sky. They had never faded—had never had a reason to fade.

"The laughter, the singing is what I miss the most." The blond-haired boy spoke again, breathing through the memories. "My grandfather made this thing—a music box, is what he called it—that filled the silence with sound."

I stopped for a second, removed my hand from the wall. "We found something like that. In a house, in the trees."

I could hear Lander walk a few steps, to the door.

"What did it look like?"

"It was small, black, with a boy and girl twirling in the middle of it. They were holding onto each other. It was…beautiful." I took a breath, thought of Theodore, the night he sang along with the box and the sound filled the black sky. "We found books too."

"Books?" He sucked in his breath. "What kind?"

"Books that were banned years ago." I looked at the others. They were staring at the wall, listening intently. "Adventures. Love stories."

I suddenly remembered something. *The picture!* The picture of the man and woman from the house. I reached in my pocket, fumbled, pulled the small white square out, breathless. "There was an album! A black album that said—"

"The Parson Family Album."

Lander and I said the words together.

I looked at the picture, at the woman in the white dress staring into the man's eyes. Holding hands like they never wanted to let go.

"You've been there?"

"I lived there."

I stepped back, hit the wall. I slid down slowly, until I reached the ground. Dalia's mouth fell open. Nash and Gavin were still staring. Alese looked at me, her eyes wide.

"Did you read them? The books?" Alese's voice rang through the room.

"Read them?" Lander chuckled again. "Only about a hundred times. I know those books, inside and out." His voice changed, grew hopeful. "Did you bring them?"

"We were going to." I thought of Arsen, wondered what he was doing out there, in the Dome. "They were burned."

"It doesn't matter anymore." Alese turned to me, her brown eyes shining. "He *knows* them, Laney! He knows the laws, the way people lived when there was love. He can help us tell the others. He can make humanity right again."

"Yes," Nash spoke suddenly, softly. His eyes stared forward, into nothing. "I can't live like this."

I thought about what he said, about what Alese had said. She was right. If there was anything I wanted, it was for the others in the Dome to experience what I had. To see colors, to smile, to laugh, to cry. To feel what I had felt. To keep it from them seemed selfish, unthinkable now. They needed it. I knew that because I had needed it. I hadn't even known what I was missing, and neither did they. They were alive, yes. But glassy eyes in a world of gray wasn't really living.

"We can't tell them."

I could hear Lander pause, could see him pressed against the smooth glass wall in my mind.

"We have to show them."

Dalia uncrossed her arms and looked at all of us. "Not to force us back to reality guys, but we're locked up."

The reality of the situation filled my mind like dirt. I started to panic.

"Lander, one of the people that was with us—he was stabbed. He's dying. He'll die if we don't help him." I looked at Alese, at the concern in her eyes. "We need to get out of here. We have to."

Lander hesitated, spoke. "Do you have anything colorful?"

I paused, confused. Our backpacks with our blankets and jackets, and the remains of the food, had been thrown in here with us. The jackets were as bright—as colorful—as day. I was surprised Mr. Dabir hadn't taken them.

"Yes."

After a moment, Lander spoke again.

"I think I might know a way. Mr. Dabir has the key, and he has to come back here to give us food." He stopped, breathed. "I've had this idea for a long time. Never really had a reason to use it until now."

I stood, my fingers cold but my cheeks flushed with warmth. "Lander, the man with black eyes that was here, he was real, wasn't he? What happened to him?"

Lander didn't respond for a long moment. Then he spoke, his words echoing on the gray walls.

"He died. Stopped eating, stopped drinking." The blond-haired boy with eyes like the ocean took a breath. "He had nothing left to destroy, so he had nothing left to live for."

36

Mr. Dabir didn't come back for two days. No one did.

It was surreal, painful, to go from a bright world with turquoise skies and grass like Theodore's green eyes to a dark room with charcoal walls, thin air, and no sound, all in less than a day. The darkness seemed to close in on us as each second passed, taunting us, threatening to cloud our eyes the moment we let our minds slip into the silence.

On the second day, I found myself wondering if love could live in a place so deeply underground and so gray that even the rock in the world above would shine in comparison. But Lander had survived. He had kept his eyes clear for a year, probably fighting the urge to let the indifference of the Dome take it each day. A whole year. Day two almost seemed like a year to me.

Alese was lying on a thin slab of rock that was pushed against the wall, like a bed. Dalia was sitting with her back against the stone, her head pressed into her fingers. Nash and Gavin were lying on the ground, their blankets underneath them, eyes staring at the ceiling. I was sitting next to them, in the place I had collapsed when Lander told us he lived in the house in the trees.

Gavin shifted, rolled to his side and unzipped his pack, taking some food out in his hand. He brought it to his mouth and chewed slowly, like he had nowhere to go. Nowhere to be. And he didn't.

"Is that the last of it?" I spoke through the silence and the sound was scratchy, hollow.

Gavin said nothing but turned to me, nodded.

I looked back at him and froze. His eyes were gray. Not gray like the people in the Dome, but clouded over with a thin mist like the one that had covered the grassy slope in the world above. His hope, his grasp on the fragments of love we had found, was slipping— and slipping fast.

He looked away and settled back on the ground, as if he hadn't noticed my eyes widening. My back stiffened and I sat up straight, suddenly more awake than I had been in hours.

"Let's do something." The words rushed from my lips and the others looked at me. Nash's eyebrows creased—he had noticed the concern in my voice.

I looked at Gavin then back at Nash. At Alese. I was at a loss for words already, not knowing what we should do. Then I remembered Theodore. The night by the water, when Nash and Arsen almost got into a fight—but Theodore had stopped them. The name competition. Relief pricked my chest as I thought of the game, of the dots of light that stared down above us in the black sky as we said names of the people from the Dome.

It worked then. It had to work now.

"Let's see how many things we can name from the world above," I said, looking at the others. At Gavin. "First one who can't think of something loses."

The four looked at me in silence. Then Nash pushed himself to his elbows and spoke.

"And what does the loser have to do?" His eyes were on me and the corner of his mouth curved, just barely. I let out a breath, but another voice came first, softly, from down the hall.

"They have to be the last to step out the door, into the world." The room became silent again.

"Lander?" I spoke to the wall, and he replied softly.

"I'm in."

I paused, but I wasn't confused. I could see why he said that, where he was going with this. To win the game, we needed to push for love. To remember every piece of it we had found with everything we had. To lose would show that we had given up, that we didn't want to remember. Because before we came back into the Dome, every one of us would have wanted to be the first to go out the thick gray door again. The question was if we still felt that way.

I looked at the others, nodded. Alese sat up, and so did Gavin. At least he still wanted to try.

"Clouds," Alese spoke, and her eyes swept over all of us, then looked at the ceiling. At what was above the ceiling. "White wisps that dotted the brilliant sky."

The game had begun.

"The sky," Nash grinned weakly, his eyes on Alese. "When we first stepped out that door—" His voice broke off. "I'll never forget it."

Dalia looked at Nash, her blue eyes still blue—still strong. "Birds." Her mouth formed into an embarrassed smile. "I'm glad they aren't dangerous."

I breathed in. The sparkling blue that turned red, purple, then black like the sky, filled my memories.

"Water."

I said nothing else, the feeling of invigoration when I jumped into the body of blue in my mind. I grasped onto it. Clutched it with all I had.

Gavin looked at the room, at the gray that stretched around us. "The canyon." His voice was empty. Broken. "It—it looked a lot like this."

Alese's eyes met mine. She understood now. She had seen too. My eyes fell.

Lander spoke from the other room like he had been waiting for this. Like the memories were on his mind every moment, so he could bring them out whenever his mind began to slip.

"My family." He paused. "Their laughs. The ridiculous things they did to make me smile. The way they looked at me, without saying a word, but I knew. I knew they loved me." He breathed. "I hope they died happy."

I stopped, and suddenly sadness overwhelmed me. This boy had love, in its purest form, but it had been snatched from him in a day. We had never had love, at least not before we went up into the world days ago. I couldn't imagine what it would be like to have something so precious that humanity sent eight of their own to the world above to find it, only to lose it. And yet somehow, Lander hadn't even lost it.

Alese's eyes were round, and she looked at the ground. I tried to think of something, anything that measured up to the love Lander had once known.

My mind was blank.

Alese looked up again, slowly, wisps of the brown hair from her bun framing her face.

"Theodore."

She whispered the word, whispered the name of the boy with red hair and green eyes that embodied innocence, emotion, and—I took in a breath—love. Theodore embodied love, didn't he? Maybe I *had* seen a piece of this love Lander had known. It was in Theodore's smile, in his eyes. In the way he was afraid yet still followed us, still stood by our side, wherever we went. Was that love? It had to be.

Nash stood slowly. He looked around the room, and then his eyes stopped on me.

"Touch," he said the word softly, and he didn't look away. "When you touch hand to hand or…" He paused, gained the courage to say what he was going to say. "Mouth to mouth."

I could feel my face flush red. Dalia looked from me to Nash and rolled her eyes, a smile tugging at her lips.

"That's called a kiss, by the way," Lander spoke from the other room, then chuckled to himself.

Nash smiled. "A kiss."

I thought of that night in the house in the trees, under the sky. A kiss. I liked the sound of that.

"Conversation." Dalia took her turn, and this time her eyes fell on the boy with dark brown hair and milky white skin. "Gavin and I had some pretty good talks up there."

Gavin looked up, surprised. His glassy eyes softened a little.

"The black box," he said the words intently, like something had tugged at the blanket over his eyes and he was starting to see again. I breathed in hard.

"It was Laney's turn," Dalia turned to Gavin and gave him a sarcastic grin.

It was, wasn't it? I didn't even care.

"So who lost, then?" Dalia looked back and forth between us.

I looked at Gavin, at the blue of his eyes, and opened my mouth to speak.

Something clicked down the hallway, then shut with a bang.

The door.

A tall man with a dark beard walked into the room, looked at all of us and narrowed his eyes in distaste.

Mr. Dabir. He was back.

37

"Well, well." Mr. Dabir spoke and we all stood. Two days was a long time. It felt strange to see him again. "Aren't we all looking splendid today?"

Splendid. The same word he had used to describe the Dome. I looked at Nash and he looked back at me, nodded slightly. I slowly unzipped my backpack.

Mr. Dabir was holding a black sheet in his hands, filled with food I guessed. He had to know we would run out of supplies soon—he must have held off for as long as he could.

"I hope you understand why it's been a few days." He looked at us, but his gray eyes held no sympathy. "Revising your plan for humanity takes time."

"What do you mean?" My hand stopped when the zipper was halfway across the pack.

"You talk too much. Ask too many questions." Mr. Dabir put his hand in his pocket, pulled out the card that opened the door. "We're letting the violent men have the world. This is our home now."

I swallowed, my throat dry. Arsen's words.

I started unzipping again, faster now. This had to work. I looked up for a second and saw the others doing the same.

When the pack was open, I reached my hand in and clutched one thing. I held it there, waiting. Watching.

Mr. Dabir pressed his card to the door and it beeped. Then the glass slid open slowly, smoothly. I could see the rustling of the man's charcoal shirt. Could hear his breath move in and out, like the Dome's vexatious lights.

Then movement rushed back into the world again.

I snapped my blanket from my pack and held it high, like the sun. Then I threw it toward the door. The others did the same, and our jackets of reds, blues, yellows, and greens whirled through the thin air and piled in a heaping mound on the floor. Right in front of Mr. Dabir.

He wasn't wearing sunglasses now.

"My eyes!"

He stepped back for a moment, his hands pressed over his face. But a moment was all we needed.

I was on my feet already, and I sprang forward. When I took the card from Mr. Dabir's hands, our fingers brushed against each other. He gasped and stumbled forward, stepped into the pile of color. He held his fingers tightly, shock written across his face, his feet frozen to the ground. It was the first time he had ever been touched.

The wall beeped and the door slid shut in front of him, the glass unable to hide the look on his face.

"Sorry, Mr. Dabir." Nash spoke, the card in his hand. He looked at the baffled man through the door. "I hope you understand."

Nash pressed the card in my hand again, and I looked at Mr. Dabir one last time, at his wide eyes, then sprinted to Lander's room. He was standing by the door, his eyes brighter than I had seen them.

When the door slid open, he hesitated for a brief moment. Then he stepped out the door and his eyes widened. He looked like we had looked when we first walked out of the Dome and into the world. I swallowed. It was his first time stepping out of the room in a year. And it was the first time I had seen him in front of the glass.

He turned and his blue eyes met mine, a smile stretched across his face. Then he spun around and ran to the room that we had been in—the room that now held a jumbled Mr. Dabir.

When Lander reached the glass door, he slowed. He pressed his hand up against the glass, his chest moving in and out, and just looked at him. Looked at the man who had locked him in this dark place, and kept him locked up here for a year.

Nash stopped, his hand on the doorknob that would lead us out of here. Gavin and Alese saw me watching and followed my gaze. Gavin reached into his backpack and pulled out his knife we had used in the world above. He walked forward and pressed it into Lander's hand. Lander looked up at the dark-haired boy for a moment and said nothing, his head turning to Mr. Dabir again.

I could hear my own breath. Swallowed. Mr. Dabir deserved to die. Locking up Lander for a year was unthinkable, cruel. As cruel as the men with black eyes.

Lander looked at the trembling man once again, crouching in the pile of jackets, and opened his mouth. Then he said one thing. But it was one thing that has played in my mind since, over and over again.

"We'll come back for you." His words were soft. Firm. "We're not going to let you die."

Then he turned, placed the knife in Gavin's hand again. His eyes fell on me, and they were radiant.

"Let's go save your friend."

My friend. I breathed in, nodded. Stilled my shaking fingers and my beating heart. Theodore was my friend.

Nash pulled and the door opened with a click. I looked at Gavin, at his dark hair and determined eyes, and at Dalia next to him, her legs bent and arms poised, ready to run. At Alese, who smiled, her eyes a clear, milky brown. At Nash, who looked back at me with intensity and softness all at the same time. Like the man looked at the woman in the white dress.

Then Nash turned and ran deeper into the world of gray, and we were right behind him.

We were breathless when we reached the door Theodore was behind. The halls were empty, and silence filled the air, but that wasn't any different from a normal day.

I put my hand on the cold, gray doorknob. I looked down the hallway once more and then turned the knob slowly, quietly, opening the door a crack. I didn't hear anyone, and I pushed it open all the way.

I stepped in and looked across the room, at the bed we had put Theodore on just days before. The sheets were pushed to the top of the mattress in a heap, the lumpy pillow on the stone floor.

"He's gone." The words tumbled from my lips to the floor and shattered. The terrifying thought crossed my mind that he might already be dead.

I looked behind me at the others and they were looking where I had looked, their eyebrows creased in concern and confusion. Alese opened her mouth to speak.

A bell reverberated through the room and I pressed my hand against the wall for balance, shaken by the sound.

Collaboration. They were meeting for their nightly Collaboration.

"We need to go," Gavin spoke, and his words sounded forced, like he didn't want to say them. He was staring at the bed.

"He's right. We need to get to Collaboration before they're all seated so we can blend in," Nash said softly.

I looked at him and he tore his eyes away and stepped into the hall. But I had seen them for a second, and they were filled with regret. Failure. Like he had let Theodore down, but more than that, like he had let all of us down.

Dalia hugged her arms around her chest and stepped out of the room, and Gavin followed slowly. Alese walked into the room and placed her hand on the bed, ran her fingers over the muted gray sheets. Then she turned, without a word, and joined them in the hall. My eyes fell on Lander, and Theodore's face flashed into my mind, his wide eyes and white cheeks when Mr. Dabir had first opened the door to the world.

"It's going to be okay."

I had said the words, not fully knowing what they meant, but Theodore had believed me. He had stilled his shaking hands, put them over his forehead to shield his eyes from the light, and stepped out the door without looking back.

I looked at Lander, at his messy blond hair and sapphire eyes.

"I told him it was going to be okay." The words left me breathless, and my chest tightened.

Lander looked back at me and his eyes didn't move, didn't look away. He looked past me, toward the hall, to the sound that was a soft tapping minutes ago and now sounded like an army, marching toward us like we were the enemy. But they didn't even know we were here. They were just walking to Collaboration, side by side, like they always had.

The boy looked back at me without a speck of gray.

"It will be."

38

I stepped out into the hallway and Dalia's blond bun spun toward us. Her eyes, usually strong, were nervous. "They're coming this way. What do we do?"

Lander stepped forward and looked down the hall, opposite from the noise. "Come on."

I looked at the others and nodded. Not trusting this boy with hair like the sun and eyes as clear as water seemed absurd.

We jogged to the other end of the hall, away from the noise, softly, so they wouldn't hear us. Lander turned left at the end of the hall instead of turning right, toward the center of the Dome where we met for Collaboration. He crouched against the stone, motioning for us to join, and we did.

We waited as the steps grew louder, the chaotic rhythm beating against the gray walls. They were right next to us now. They had to be.

When the first row of people turned the corner, their backs toward us as they walked the other way, I sucked in my breath. Then another row passed, and another. Silent breaths and still hands with only one place to go, and one place to be. Their cloudy eyes were focused on going to Collaboration. They hadn't even noticed us.

Lander turned, his eyes on us again. He held up his hand and then brought one finger down at a time. Slowly.

Five. Four. Three. Two.

I looked out at the sea of lifeless faces.

One.

We stepped behind the last row and fell into pace with the rest.

No one stopped. I breathed in, but I didn't turn my head. No one turned their heads while in line. I needed to blend in—to be one of them again.

Walking to Collaboration in a straight line, with the rest of the people in the Dome, felt too familiar. I remembered the silence. Feeling like I was alone even though I was in the middle of a crowd. I had known this was my world, and I had been content with it.

I pushed my shaking hands into my pockets and clutched the photograph of the man and woman from the house in the trees. Would I have wanted to change my world if a group of teenagers showed me a picture?

"We need to show them," Lander had said back in the hall, when we were locked up. Well, this was something to show. We had all agreed. This was the proof Mr. Dabir had wanted. If this didn't change their minds, nothing would.

We reached the center of the Dome and I held my breath as we walked through the door. Ms. Geena moved from her position in line to the platform. I closed my eyes for a second, relieved. Mr. Dabir wasn't scheduled to head Collaboration today.

I didn't stop looking forward as I took my seat. If anyone noticed our eyes, we would be discovered. They would know it was us. For the first time, I was thankful we all had to wear the same dismal clothes and tight buns. Unless someone was looking closely, we all appeared the same.

"Let us begin."

Ms. Geena placed her clipboard on the podium and nodded at someone in the audience. I watched, creased my eyebrows. Normally the person leading Collaboration called each person by name and waited to see if they had any new idea or memory about the humanity before our time and then it would be voted into law. It was the same, every night for thirteen years.

Someone in the sea of people shifted, stood.

Arsen.

His back was to me, but I knew it was him. I had walked behind him for days, and I knew the back of his head like I knew the world above. He looked back once as he walked, and I blinked. His sunglasses were gone. His dark eyes swept the crowd, and they were brooding.

Ms. Geena straightened as Arsen walked to the center of the people, stepped onto the podium, and took the microphone from her fingers. I didn't even slide down in my seat—if I knew Arsen, he didn't care about anyone but himself. He wouldn't notice us— needles in a haystack.

"Mr. Dabir has agreed that we should stay in the Dome," Arsen's voice rang out, echoed around the room.

No one moved. Apparently they hadn't told the others about their "revised plan for humanity" yet. I watched him silently.

"I know some of you may have been told otherwise, but we're not running out of supplies." Arsen's eyes swept the crowd, narrowed slightly. "That was a lie created by the teachers because one of our own had changed for the worse—Adrian, they called him. And they were worried you would all change too. Or he would kill us. Either way."

My arm moved, clutched the side of my seat. That was why the teachers had sent us above. They were terrified we were all going to learn to hate too. Just like Adrian. I shut my eyes.

"But they were lying. I searched this place up and down for their *so-called Adrian*. He doesn't exist."

Adrian died! I wanted to scream out the words. Tell the people the truth. But I couldn't.

"Your beloved teachers lied to you not once, but twice," Arsen spat the words. "And why? Well—" a noise erupted from his lips that almost sounded like a snicker—"it doesn't really matter anymore, does it?"

Ms. Geena's eyes widened and she took a step back. Arsen saw her and his mouth twisted slightly.

"So I guess our first order of business is to take a vote. All in favor of locking up the teachers for breaking our law of 'honesty at all times'?"

Arsen looked out at the audience. The silence was excruciating. No one shifted, no one moved. These teachers had given us knowledge, helped us create this world with new laws and peace for thirteen years. They were all the people knew; they would be lost without them.

Ms. Geena stepped forward again, smoothed her shirt. Her hands were shaking.

Arsen's eyes lowered, disappointed.

"All right then."

He folded his arms, looked out at the crowd.

"Next order of business. Mr. Dabir wanted proof that the men with black eyes still exist up there. Said it wasn't fair—wasn't equal to all—if he didn't believe the rest of the eight that went above ground, but he believed me." He took a breath. "But that's not a problem. I told him I have proof. And I do."

Arsen's eyes crept over us and then fell on the door that led into this room. It was closed, the thick slab of gray a cork in the Dome's center.

"Here's your proof, Mr. Dabir."

I heard the door swing open, but I didn't turn. Couldn't. No one else would. I heard footsteps—someone walking through the door to the platform. Two people. Then one of the people gasped in air, started coughing. The people stopped walking. The sound filled the air and made me cringe.

My eyes were on Arsen. His mouth twitched as he tried not to grin. He stood up straighter, his eyes unmoving as he watched whatever was coming down the aisle. He looked different, strange. Almost—pleased with himself.

I stared straight ahead, my heart beating in my chest, when the people started moving again. Started walking toward the center, toward the guy with eyes like the night sky.

I blinked when the first person started to come into view. A woman—old, gray hair, wrinkled skin. I clutched the seat again. The woman from the Dome? The woman who had winked at me. But what was she doing there, and not in the audience?

She was walking in front of the other person, and slowly, I began to see the outline of the person behind her. The features. A boy.

He stopped again, heaved in the Dome's cold air through his lungs. Then he took another step. And another.

Gray clothes. Small in stature. Thin. Red hair.

I froze. *Red hair.*

I did everything I could to keep from standing, from running to the boy who was struggling down to the podium in the middle of the crowd of glassy-eyed people. My heart beat faster. Sweat beaded my neck.

It was Theodore.

39

When Theodore reached the front, he turned toward us. His chest was sucking in air, his hair ruffled on his head. A blanket was still wrapped tightly around his stomach, and what had once been blood was now dry. He was still struggling, was still gasping for air every few seconds, but he was standing. Walking, if you could call it that. He looked…better. How was that possible?

Theodore put his hand against the podium to support himself, and when he did, he looked up. His eyes were pools of green, as bright as they were in the world above, if not more than that. He had held onto it—through the pain, after being stabbed by the very person who was in front of him now—he had held onto the reality of love. A face flashed into my mind. The woman I had seen behind the window when I was taken to the Dome. Her clear, heartbroken eyes—holding onto love when the world was chaos around her.

Theodore's eyes were searching, sifting through the audience row by row, seat by seat. Frantically. He was looking for us.

"Theodore and Delma," Arsen spoke, and his eyes never left the boy in front of him. Theodore stopped searching and tore his eyes from the crowd, looked back at him. What was Delma doing with Theodore?

"Delma, let's start with you." Arsen paced the platform slowly, but the old woman didn't move. Her eyes were soft but strong. She didn't look afraid.

"*I said* back up." Arsen turned from Delma and looked at Theodore, his voice raising. Theodore took a step back. "Good." Arsen breathed again, looked at Delma, then out at all of us.

"As you all know, Theodore was injured. Well, *is* injured." Arsen held back a smirk. "And this woman"—He pointed to Delma. She stared back, unblinking—"was found helping him. Trying to heal him, if you will."

My eyes widened. She was helping him? That explained why he could stand—why he looked better. She broke the law to help someone she didn't even know?

"And we all know that's breaking one of our laws," Arsen continued. "'What is done is done for the good of *all* the people.'" Arsen stopped pacing, looked out at the people. "All in favor of locking up this woman for breaking the law we set firmly in place thirteen years ago?"

The room grew silent again. I sat back in my seat. If they didn't lock up the teachers for lying, there was no way they would—

I blinked. Someone stood.

Arsen nodded, acknowledging the person in the audience. Then he stepped back. Waited. Another person in the sea of people shifted, clutched the arm of her chair, and slowly stood to her feet. Then another. And another.

I watched, horrified. Only seconds had passed, and half of the people were on their feet. They didn't turn their heads, didn't say a word. They just stared straight ahead, their eyes on the woman who had saved Theodore's life.

When almost all of the people were standing, Nash nudged my arm gently. I turned my head slightly, and his eyes were large, full of regret. Then he stood to his feet.

Nash was voting with them? My heart burned in my chest, my mind was numb, confused.

Then Dalia stood, slowly. Gavin followed, and Alese smoothed her shirt and stood up next to him. Lander was last, his hands in his pockets, his head looking down at the floor.

I looked at them all, taken aback. Furious. What were they doing?

Alese's eye caught mine, and she shook her head slowly. Her brown eyes were wide.

I stopped. *They would know.* If we were the only ones to vote against Delma being locked up, they would know who we were. That we were here. Our plan would be ruined before it had even started.

My hands were trembling as I placed my feet firmly on the ground, took a breath, and pushed. When I was standing I looked down, at the ground. At anyone but Delma. I couldn't bear to see her face. Our plan had to work now. It had to.

"I'm glad we're all in agreement," Arsen's voice stabbed the silence. "Take her away."

I heard someone walk forward, and then two people walking away from us, toward the door. I looked up once more and I saw her face before she turned and walked out of the Dome, escorted by one of the teachers. Her eyes were large, pools of gray and blue, but she didn't blink, didn't show regret. She didn't deserve this. I clenched my fists. She was the only person in here that still had a heart.

"They're going to find Mr. Dabir," Nash whispered the words under his breath. "This has to happen fast."

The realization hit me as soon as he said it. He was right. They were going to find Mr. Dabir locked up, and they weren't going to find us. This needed to happen now.

"All right, now to the real reason we're all here." Arsen spoke, louder than before.

I slid my hand into my pocket, grabbed the photograph in my fingertips, and pulled it out, my eyes still staring forward. Arsen kept talking.

"This, ladies and gentlemen, Mr. Dabir, is your proof. Your proof of the men with black eyes." He swept his arm toward the boy like he was introducing him in a grandeur way.

I let my hand drop, tried to swallow. Arsen was going to use Theodore's injuries as proof of the men with black eyes. The injuries *he* had caused. This wasn't right. It had never been right. I clutched the photograph firmly again, passed it slowly to Nash.

"Look at his eyes."

What? My hand froze next to Nash's.

Arsen motioned to the boy. Waited.

"Face them, Theodore!"

Theodore did nothing. He didn't turn his eyes away from Arsen, didn't move.

Arsen breathed out, frustration filling his face. He stopped, uncrossed his arms, walked the few steps to Theodore, and kicked him in the back of the legs.

"I said face them!"

Theodore gasped and fell to his knees, his hands spread out before him. He lifted his head slowly, his face twisted in pain, and when he did, I saw his eyes. We all saw his eyes. No one in the audience moved. I didn't understand. His eyes were green, not black. Not like the violent people.

Nash took the picture from my hand and slowly passed it to Gavin. He pressed it into Dalia's hands, who passed it to Alese. They were all watching in disbelief.

"Don't you see?" Arsen looked out at the people, watched their faces. "He's one of them!"

I wanted to turn to Nash, wanted to look at anyone else in the sea of people around me. To see if they saw what I saw. To see if they were as confused as me. I saw Alese place the photo in Lander's hands out of the corner of my eye. I took a breath. This was it. Now the people with lifeless eyes would see. After thirteen years, they would finally see the proof of love.

"This is what the world above does to you." Arsen was breathing faster now, his eyes darting into the crowd. "It turns you into one of them. There's no love to be found up there, or anywhere." He breathed more slowly. His eyes narrowed. "It disappeared when we did, thirteen years ago."

Lander whispered something to the person next to him, a thin man with graying hair and pale skin. Then he handed him the photograph of the man and woman staring into each other's eyes. Lander's grandparents.

At first, the man did nothing. Continued to stare straight ahead, his cloudy eyes unmoving. Then he looked down, so slowly, so carefully he must have thought the slight movement might break his neck.

He took the photograph in his fingers, looked at it for a second. Then he passed it to the person next to him.

"The world above is a disgusting place," Arsen's voice swam through the air above us. "It has trees, water, color—so much color." He shuddered.

I turned my head slightly, looked down the row of people. The man had passed the photograph to a woman with blond hair, who had passed it to another woman with long fingers. She glanced at it, then passed it to the tall man next to her. He held the photograph in his fingertips and placed it on the lap of the person next to him.

He hadn't even looked at it.

I swallowed hard, and my heart beat faster. They weren't even looking. *They weren't even looking.*

"It has so many things that should have been destroyed, and stayed destroyed."

Arsen's sentence made me stop. Tear my eyes from the people on our row and look up at him. What he just said sounded familiar—too familiar.

He stepped off the platform, walked into the aisle, and stood, unmoving. He was just a few feet from me, and his eyes moved slowly over the crowd.

And then I saw them. The blood drained out of my head.

Without love, the good, the beauty in this life suddenly seemed ugly. And everything that was dirty, destructive, and lifeless suddenly seemed beautiful.

Now I knew why he thought the world was horrifying. Why he said Theodore's eyes were black. It's because his were.

40

Before I was taken to the Dome, in the moments between my mother's death and my descent down the long, gray stairs, I had to walk through a world that was being destroyed right before my eyes.

It was almost dreamlike, stepping past broken stems of flowers and piles of dead leaves, hearing the moans and shrieks of people that you knew were not going to make it. I don't remember much from my journey through death to life.

But I remember him.

He was tall, strong, no older than eighteen, brown hair that fell over his forehead and a face that had once grasped the world but had lost it all.

He was standing on the dirty streets, a pile of glass by his feet. He wasn't doing anything at first, just standing in the middle of the dirt, staring out at the chaos. But he was the one who made the woman with deep brown eyes by the window turn away in fear.

His eyes were round, scared, pools of gray mixed with blue, like the sky had once been. He turned in a circle, slowly taking in the world around him. The muted sun that hid behind the dark clouds of smoke. The white buildings of stone that crumbled to the ground when fire devoured the walls. The angry men who yelled terrible things and then laughed, their eyes wild, as they pulled grass from a field and threw it on top of the ashes. The child who clung to a broken doll as tears ran in fitful sheets down her face.

The boy with blond hair collapsed to his knees, the dirt pressed against his dark blue pants. He took his face in his hands and shook his head, must have wondered for a brief moment what had happened to the world. What had happened to humanity.

Then he planted his hand firmly on the ground. He stood slowly, his body trembling, his chest pulling in what was left of the thick air. He looked up, and his eyes met mine. The gray, the specks of blue, were gone. They were black, like the smoke that was spiraling into the sky.

In less than a minute, he had made his choice. And in less than a week, Arsen had made his.

Arsen was turning slowly, staring out at the world around him like the boy from the world above had done. Staring out at the people with gray eyes, his eyes the most lifeless of them all.

"Do you hear me? Love does not exist!" He yelled the words and they echoed around the room. Stabbed me in the heart.

"And any piece of this world above does not belong down here. In our world." He was heaving in deep breaths now. His eyes darted across the room, off the thick gray walls, and landed on the boy with red hair. On Theodore.

The photograph was at a standstill, frozen in a man's hand in the row in front of us. They had been passing it quickly now, without glancing down to see what it was. Passing it like it was something Ms. Geena had asked for that needed to get from the back of the room to the front. Our plan wasn't working, and I didn't know what to do.

The walls in the Dome seemed thick, darker than usual. I clutched the edge of my seat and it felt cold. I breathed in, glanced around me at the faces that were watching with no expression, watching without a care in the world. For a brief second, they seemed almost normal. Like they were the perfect picture of humanity and I was the crazy one.

I thought of my mother, of the way her eyes had fallen, the way her hair had floated gently down to her face when the bullet hit her chest. The men with black eyes had killed her simply because she was there. Simply because she had eyes that were speckled with dots of gray and brown, eyes that were not black like theirs. Maybe if she had black eyes she would have had more of a chance, at least until the violent people started to destroy each other. We could have escaped together. She would still be with me today.

I took a deep, shaky breath. No. Black eyes were death. I would never want her to become one of them.

I sat in my chair, clutching the memories of the world above. I couldn't become one of them again. I had to help them become like me. But the sinking realization that I had never seen gray eyes become clear down here, in the Dome, was creeping into my mind. I had only seen the opposite happen—with the dark-haired man named Adrian. With Arsen. What if it wasn't possible? What if love didn't live underground? What if the only way to show these people love was to bring them through the door?

I felt the hope draining from my eyes. Felt my mind slipping back into the world of the Dome, and I desperately tried to keep it out.

"Laney," Nash said my name, the word barely passing his lips so no one around us would hear.

I didn't look up. I was sinking into my thoughts like the way I had sunk into the dull walls of the Dome. Like the way I had sunk into this world without love.

"I live in a world where love does not exist." I could just hear the sentence pass over my tongue. The words were a whisper, and they swam through the air slowly.

That was how it all started, wasn't it? A world where love did not exist. And now here we were, no better off than we had been thirteen years ago, even after eight of us had journeyed through the world above.

"What?" Nash had heard the words pass over my lips, but he didn't look at me. His eyes were on the platform. I could see his arm tense up next to mine.

I wanted to touch his arm, to grasp his hand again, to remember. But they would notice. The world above the Dome seemed distant now, like a breath of wind that skimmed across the body of blue water. I searched my memories, clung to the thought of that water, grasped it as hard as I could. My mind was slipping, like Gavin's had. I couldn't let it slip. And yet the thought of going back to a world with no worry and no pain seemed comforting for a moment. More comforting than this. But that was the lie they had created so we would be content with this life of gray walls. Wasn't it?

Nash was still watching the platform, his eyebrows creased in concern. In fear.

I swallowed. My heart was hammering in my chest. I thought of the photograph, of Lander's grandparents. Of the hands that passed it without a second thought. I thought of the world, of the destruction. I had seen a woman who still clung to love in the window thirteen years ago. But love had lost, and hate—violence—had won. It had lost seventy-four years ago too, when we voted it out of existence. What made today any different?

I breathed in deeply, stilled my trembling fingers. Let the words I was thinking cross my lips.

"Nash." I paused. Drew in a shaky breath. "What if we can't win?"

What if it was a war I couldn't overcome? A war my mother had died trying. I had never seen love win before—had only seen it destroyed time and time again.

This time Nash heard me, and he turned, opened his mouth to say something back. But before he could answer, before he could say anything, there was a loud sound in the center of the room. A thump, and then a crash.

Nash tore his eyes away from mine and I followed his gaze. I blinked.

Theodore was lying on the ground, his arms stretched out in front of him. Arsen was standing above him, seething, his eyes as black as the sky had been when the world was destroyed. He was holding a knife in his dirty hand.

I didn't move, didn't breathe. I watched, like the rest of the people with lifeless eyes.

41

Nash clenched the chair with both fists. Stared at the boy with black hair and black eyes, ready to spring up at a moment's notice.

I braced my hands on the chair's arms. I knew I needed to help too—to save this innocent boy who believed in love without a second thought. But was it worth it?

I shuddered at the thought that had crossed through my mind, at the fact that I had let it.

If we fought for love, the fighting would never end. The screaming, being locked up in rooms of glass, would be our reality, day after day. I didn't know if I could take it.

I clenched my fingers in my hand.

We could still survive if we became content with gray eyes and silence. It may not be the world above, but it was enough. It had to be enough. It would be a life without the promise of death. The people down here didn't want to change. They didn't even try. And even if they did, change down here might not even be possible. I had lost my mother in this fight, this war. I didn't want to lose my friends too.

I thought of Nash, of the kiss in the house in the trees. Of the way his hand had pressed into my back. My eyes fell, and I clutched my shirt, saw him breathe out of the corner of my eye. We may not be able to touch anymore, but at least he wouldn't die. At least he would be here. As much as you could call silence and no touch "being here." I had lived without it for eighteen years, after all. It would be worth it. It had to be.

Arsen was standing over Theodore, a grin twisted on his cheeks. The people were watching, their lips closed, their eyes unblinking. They didn't even seem surprised.

"People like you don't belong down here, Theodore." He cringed when he said the boy's name. "You're everything that's wrong with this world." He stepped closer, held the knife higher. "I should have finished you in the trees."

Nash pressed his feet to the ground, lifted his hands from the chair and began to stand. My eyes widened. Arsen would kill Nash too.

"Stop!"

I cringed when I heard the sound. The voice. Nash froze, his head turned. It wasn't him.

The doors to the center of the Dome opened with a thud and Mr. Dabir came crashing through, followed by the person who had locked Delma up. His face was red, his black beard shaking back and forth in anger.

He walked to the front of the platform and didn't pause to smooth his shirt.

Arsen turned and his eyes fell on Mr. Dabir. He looked annoyed that he had been interrupted. Theodore looked exhausted, and he pushed to his knees. Relief rushed to his green eyes. But Mr. Dabir didn't even look at him. When he reached the center of the room, he whipped around, toward the people.

"The six we locked up have escaped! They're among you now." He peered into the audience. "Find them."

Sweat beaded my neck, but I pretended not to notice. It was all over now, before it had even begun. Love had lost again—maybe it was inevitable.

When the man in front of us turned, his eyes widened slightly. He said nothing but simply stood, pointed to our row. Pointed to Alese, Dalia, Gavin, Lander, Nash, and me.

Mr. Dabir's eyes followed the man's hand and he breathed in deeply, then stepped from the platform. He nodded slightly to four men that were seated on either side of the audience. Four of the teachers. They stood and fell into step behind Mr. Dabir, clenching their fists as they did.

I didn't want the others to fight back, didn't want them to risk creating even more chaos. So I stood up, my eyes on Mr. Dabir, and held my hands above my chest.

I could feel Nash's eyes widen, could see Alese's face fall in disappointment. Where there was no war, there were no casualties. And the war wasn't worth it.

Mr. Dabir didn't stop walking, but his eyes fell on me. On my eyes. He looked at them for a moment too long. "Well, at least one of you has some sense again."

I didn't move, looked away from Mr. Dabir, at anything else. My eyes fell on Theodore. He was kneeling on the floor, his eyes wide, unblinking. I tried to look away, but I couldn't. Then something filled his eyes, something I had seen when he was standing on the stage that first night at Collaboration, tears in his voice as he sang his mother's song.

Grief. Disbelief.

I swallowed. He was just now realizing we had been there all along, in the audience of gray eyes, and we had done nothing to help him.

But this would help him. As long as we stayed silent, no one would be killed. Mr. Dabir wouldn't allow it.

Something touched my hand. I tore my eyes away, looked down. A rope. Mr. Dabir wrapped it around my wrists and tightened the ends. I looked down the row. He had done the same to the others. It was so they wouldn't have to touch us.

He pulled the rope and my knees buckled. I staggered to the end of the row. Nash was in front of me and he turned his head, looked into my eyes with confusion. Then his eyes flashed and he turned back, walked forward without a word.

"This is the only way," I said to Nash, my words desperate, my voice shaking.

I turned to Mr. Dabir, my eyes on the back of his head. "Theodore's on the platform. You need to tie him up too."

Mr. Dabir stopped walking. Spun around slowly. "Theodore?" His eyes swept past me and fell on the boy with red hair. "As far as I'm concerned, he's already dead."

The words hit my chest. I stepped backward without realizing it. A grin tugged at Mr. Dabir's lips.

"And dead people aren't for the good of us all, are they?"

I watched in horror as he nodded to Arsen, and Arsen nodded back. Then Mr. Dabir spun around again, toward the door.

I stood in a daze, my feet rooted to the stone floor. The others were struggling, trying to get loose, but Mr. Dabir's men were strong. And we had been in a cell for two days.

Alese was pulling against the rope and she turned and looked at Theodore. Her brown eyes were wide, terrified. Gavin was breathing heavy, frantic breaths, the confidence all but gone from his face, the memory of the black box a fragment of a thought. Nash whipped around and pulled, caught the man holding the rope by surprise. In one swift movement, he pushed his fingers from the knot and pulled one hand free.

Mr. Dabir stopped, retrieved a black metal rod from his pocket, and smashed it into Nash's shoulder. Nash cried out and fell to his knees, clutching his arm. He staggered back to his feet when the men started pulling him down the aisle again.

I watched in disbelief. Glanced at the people around us, the tight skin with perfect buns. They stared back. It was the world again, thirteen years ago, coming to life before my eyes. The people with black eyes may be murderers, but the people with eyes as gray as the clouds were just as bad. They watched it all happen. They *let* it happen.

I blinked. Breathed in, then out again. A woman seated a few feet away watched me, her blond bun frozen in place. Her eyes met mine. Beneath the gray, beneath the sheet that covered them, was something else. What was it?

I searched my thoughts, searched my memory. I stopped. Mr. Dabir's words. The words he had spoken before we went out the Dome's door.

"But many of the people down here..." He stopped. His hands went to his hair. "Are terrified. They don't remember a life without murder, without destruction. More than just making sure the world is safe now, our people need to be convinced. They need to want to go above ground. To believe in it. Otherwise our community will fall, and humans will cease to exist."

I froze. *Fear.*

Fear was the root of it all. Just as the boy with blond hair had stared at the world before he decided to be a part of it. It wasn't anger that drove the men with black eyes and the people with gray eyes to do what they did. It wasn't hatred, or fury, or pain.

It was fear.

Fear was an emotion so powerful that when people allowed it to take over, it chased compassion out of their hearts. Out of their eyes.

I sucked in my breath, looked at Theodore, horrified. They weren't going to let us live in peace, even if we didn't fight back. We were different from them now, and that terrified them. And as long as they were terrified, our lives were as good as over. Theodore's life was as good as over.

If I didn't fight, I was dead. The thought alone was enough to penetrate my eyes and give new purpose to my mind. To my heart.

The war was inevitable. We had started it when we walked back through the Dome's door with eyes like the sun.

42

The next time Mr. Dabir looked away, his eyes on the front of the taciturn room, I yanked the rope as hard as I could.

It slipped through his fingers, the rough edges rubbing against his pale skin, and he let out a cry. But it worked. I was free.

I caught the stunned look on Nash's face just before I spun around, sucked in air, and bolted for Theodore. I was a few steps from the front, Arsen's eyes widening in surprise, when I jolted backward, the force of the pull resonating through my bones, my nerves. I fell to my knees, the pain shooting through me, and looked up.

Mr. Dabir had stepped on it. He had stepped on the rope that was still tied to my hands.

"Mr. Dabir, this isn't right!" I tried to speak, choked the words. "You wanted love, remember? This isn't love. You can't kill him."

Mr. Dabir bent slowly, picked up the rope, and wrapped it around his hand a few times before he clenched the end of it tightly. He looked up, at me.

"Love does not exist anymore, Laney." The words came from his lips, as smooth as butter. "You proved that when you returned from above, just as crazy as the men with black eyes."

"It's a different crazy! A good crazy." I was frantic, gasped for air. "Just give us a chance."

"The day I give that thing you call love a chance is the day I condemn this world we have built for *thirteen years* to death." He wrapped the rope around his hand once more. Blinked. "And all this time I thought love would save humanity. I can see why they banned it now."

Mr. Dabir straightened and his eyes looked past me, to Arsen. "Finish him quickly."

"No. Please." My heart sunk deep into my chest. Bile formed at the back of my throat. "No. Please no!"

"It's too late, Laney." Mr. Dabir spun once more, said the words firmly. His patience was running thin. "You can't fight us anymore. It's you"—he swept his arm around the room full of people with glassy eyes—"against all of us. Who do you think's going to win?"

An image flashed into my mind. It was just for a moment, a picture of Nash and me, standing in front of the people at Collaboration. My feet were rooted to the ground, waiting, in silence. My cloudy eyes and muted mind were used to the quiet, the cold air, the gray, and I looked out at the people in front of me thinking, knowing that they were my people. That I was like them, and they were like me. Thinking that was how life was supposed to be.

And then Nash had touched me.

He had held my hand up for the world to see. And that moment—I blinked, trying to focus on Mr. Dabir, the others—that moment had proved to me that there was something else. It had taken away my fear, if just for a second. It had changed everything for me.

It had changed me.

I stood slowly, the sudden silence pressing down on me.

"You're right." I paused. Breathed. "We can't win."

Mr. Dabir didn't look away. His eyes were searching mine, searching for the truth of my statement. He blinked once, seemed satisfied, and started to turn his head to the door again.

"But love can," I said the words firmly, calmly, but with more confidence than I had ever said anything before.

Theodore looked up and his green eyes flashed with surprise. Nash turned his head, caught my eye. A smile curved on the corners of his lips. Mr. Dabir whipped around, but it was too late. I had already given the order with my eyes—used them for something more than just staring at a gray world.

At the same time, Nash and I stomped on the foot of the person who was holding our rope. The man next to Nash stepped back in pain, in the shock of being touched for the first time in his life. Mr. Dabir's eyes opened, wide, and he reeled back in disgust. To feel the warmth of another was like touching fire, and he didn't want to get burnt.

Nash pulled the rope free from his hands and turned to the others—to Dalia and Alese, Gavin and Lander—and I started to do the same.

"Laney, go!"

Nash's eyes were on the platform in the center of the room, and his face was white.

I spun around, my gaze following his, and froze.

Arsen was standing over Theodore, pulling the knife from the boy's leg. He had tried to stab him, but Theodore had moved—he had moved just enough. Arsen was panicking. His window of opportunity had just gotten smaller, and he knew it.

I gasped, sucked in a deep, cold breath, and ran.

I could see the eyes in the audience turning, moving slowly as they followed me down the aisle. But I knew I didn't have to worry about them coming to Arsen's aid. Sitting silently and watching the world pass by was their job. It was their life.

"Arsen!"

I reached the platform, hurdled the edge, and slammed into the boy with dark hair and dark eyes. He fell to Theodore's side, his eyes widening, and the knife clattered to the ground next to me. Arsen pushed himself to his elbows and looked up. His eyes fell on the smooth silver blade.

I looked down, my shoulder writhing in pain, and kicked it away. It slid under some seats behind us. The people in them didn't move.

Arsen's eyes narrowed and he jumped to his feet again, but I beat him to it. I stepped in front of the boy with green eyes and red hair and stopped, planted my feet firmly, gasped the words that were in my mind, and on my heart.

"You're going to have to get through me first."

Arsen paused, and I saw confusion fill his eyes for a split second. He stepped forward, then stepped back. He didn't have the knife anymore. He would have to touch me with his bare hands to get to Theodore. And that terrified him. Mallory had died holding firmly to the "touch is forbidden" rule. Would he?

"Give me the knife!" Arsen looked frantically toward the people with gray eyes. They didn't move. He looked back at me, then stopped. In one motion he sprang forward, sprinted around me, and moved toward Theodore.

I moved quickly and stepped in front of Theodore's other side before he did, barely. A surge of fear hammered my chest. He was trying to get past me by moving around me. I wasn't enough. One person wasn't enough.

Suddenly I felt a hand thread its fingers into mine, and the warmth rushed through me like water. I looked beside me.

Nash.

Alese ran toward us, breathless, and clutched my other hand. Gavin and Dalia were sprinting from the end of the aisle toward us. I looked behind them. The men that were helping Mr. Dabir weren't there anymore. They had fled. And where was Mr. Dabir?

Dalia grasped Alese's hand, and Gavin took hold of Dalia's. We were forming a circle around Theodore—a circle around the gray platform. I looked behind me, at the others. There was a gap. The platform was large, and five people weren't enough. I blinked.

We needed more.

Arsen was standing, inching toward the opening with his black eyes on Theodore.

"Help us!" I yelled the words, frantic. The people in the audience—the sea of gray eyes and pale skin—didn't move. They didn't even acknowledge that they had heard me.

"Please," I pleaded.

"What are you guys doing?" The voice came from behind me, tired, confused. Concerned. I turned. Theodore. He was trying to push himself to his elbows, and my eyes met his—green. Pure, innocent, emerald green.

Nash turned next to me and his hand squeezed mine.

"You asked what a family was once." He paused. "We're your family, Theodore."

Theodore stopped, looked at Nash. He stared for a moment. Then his lips moved, slowly, and he smiled. Despite the pain, despite the wounds, he smiled. Then he whispered four words that took my breath away. Four words I have never heard before. And four words I will never forget.

"I love you guys."

43

Arsen stepped back and his face twisted in disgust. He clenched his fists next to his body and I could see his hands. Trembling. Trembling from the fury of what Theodore had said.

He took a step forward, braced himself to crash through the opening, when a sound pierced the silence. A voice. I looked around, at Nash, at Alese. But it wasn't them. It wasn't any of us.

It came from the sea of gray eyes.

"Where did you hear that word?" It was the voice of a man. Quiet, but clear. Scratchy at the edges from years of not having to talk. Of not wanting to.

I squinted, looked out into the people. Paused, to make sure I had heard right. The room was silent.

"Love?"

Something in the audience shifted. Then someone stood, slowly, carefully, like he had years of age on his hands. The man had gray hair and light gray eyes that faded to mint blue at the edges. Wrinkles stretched across his face.

"No." He stared at us. His eyes fell on Nash. "Family."

Nash didn't speak for a moment. He was looking at the man, confused. Probably because the silence—the audience of gray eyes—had spoken for the first time. It was unexpected.

"We found it on a book in the trees," Nash said, choosing his words carefully. He looked at Arsen, then back at the man. "In a house."

The older man's eyes widened. He took a half step forward, clutched the seat in front of him. "I used to have a family. Seventy-five years ago."

The man's face brightened. Something tugged at the blanket over his eyes as he remembered—as memories from the time that was forbidden flooded his mind. His eyes softened, and they settled on us again.

"I will help you."

I watched, frozen, as the man looked to his right, down the row, and began walking to the aisle. He passed the frozen buns and tight lips, carefully stepping over their feet as he did. One woman turned as he passed. Her eyes followed him for a few seconds before she set her eyes forward again and stared straight ahead.

When the man reached us, he stepped up on the platform, placing a hand on each knee for support. He walked over to Gavin and lifted his hand, trembling with old age.

"What's your name?" Nash spoke, and his eyes never left the man. Didn't blink.

The gray head turned, looked back at us before he plunged his hand into Gavin's and added one more person to the circle. One more person in the fight for love.

"Alfred." He paused, thought a moment. "Alfred Porter."

I breathed in. He had a last name too. Just like the Parsons. That must have been something humanity did when love existed—they named their families. A smile tugged at my cheeks. I liked the idea.

Arsen was standing in shock, his eyes circling all of us. Circling the people in the audience.

Then someone else in the ocean of gray stood.

I turned, and my eyes fell on a woman with a black bun that was graying at the edges. She opened her mouth to speak.

"I was only three when love was banned." She looked down at the floor, smoothed her shirt slowly. "But the memories—they come back to me sometimes." She paused, coughed once from the difficulty of talking, then looked up again. "But this—this is more like my memories than anything I've seen down here. I remember my family. And families—" She stopped, breathed in deeply, slowly. "Families would stick together."

She stood there for a moment, staring. She breathed in a single, shaky breath and released her fingers from the chair's back in front of her, white from clutching it anxiously. Then she started walking down her row.

While she was walking past the people in gray, and when she reached the center aisle, another person stood. It was a woman with gray hair like the Dome and long fingers. One more stood after her, another man, his back stooped over with age. He walked so slowly that necks turning to watch him pass didn't even seem to move. But when he reached us, he grasped the hand of the person at the end of the line—the woman with gray hair—with strength. Purpose.

Arsen stepped back. His eyes were as wide as the cold, gray door to the Dome.

The sea of gray stilled, and I looked out at the people. Four had stood. Four with gray hair and gray eyes. They remembered— somewhere deep in their minds they remembered a fragment of love, a family.

The others didn't have these memories. They remained seated in the midst of the movement. They watched, eyes unmoving and lips pressed firmly together. Distrust—fear—was rooted deeply in their hearts, and they were clinging to it with all they had. Maybe because it was all they had.

I looked over at Nash, and he was watching them. Warmth rushed through me and I squeezed his fingers. Maybe love could exist in this cold, gray world. He turned in surprise and his eyes met mine. He smiled.

Arsen wasn't moving. His eyes were on all of us, wide, nervous. He blinked. Four of his people had turned against him—the wall of gray eyes had cracked. And he didn't know what to do.

The door to the Dome's center swung open and I tore my eyes from Arsen. My heart stopped. For a split second, I forgot the warmth, forgot the people clutching each other's hands after seventy-four years. Forgot Nash's smile.

Mr. Dabir was standing in the open door, unmoving. And in front of him, with a knife held to his neck, was Lander.

Lander.

My hand pressed into Nash's and I felt dizzy. How could I have forgotten?

Everyone on the platform stopped. Didn't breathe. Their eyes—now a little less gray—were on the boy with blond hair and blue eyes.

The room was silent again.

Mr. Dabir paused for a moment and looked around in confusion, bewilderment. Then he straightened, clutched the knife even tighter. "This boy was going to break Delma out, but I stopped him." His eyes swept the platform. Lingered over the wrinkled faces. "Just in time, apparently."

Lander tried to move, but Mr. Dabir held the knife closer to his neck, tighter. Mr. Dabir cringed and lifted his hand from Lander's arm for a moment. He was touching him. He was touching him, and he didn't seem to care.

Lander stopped struggling, looked at the platform for the first time—at the four gray heads that grasped our hands tightly. His mouth parted and his face brightened. Disbelief. Excitement.

A little piece of his world—the world with love—was standing right in front of his eyes.

Mr. Dabir straightened again, looked at Arsen, who was standing like stone in the corner. Then his eyes fell on us again. Fell on me.

"Let go of your hands." His voice was low. Calm. "Or I will kill him."

The room came to a standstill. Silence pounded the air. But no one moved.

I turned to Nash, and he looked back at me. I saw Alese, the torture in her eyes. Saw Dalia take a small step back, into the circle. The people around me stood still, unmoving. Their eyes turned to me.

If we let go, we were letting go of everything that had just happened. We were letting go of love. I breathed in and felt the cool air fill my lungs.

But we had to. It wouldn't be love if we watched someone die. I wouldn't be one of them anymore. I wouldn't be someone with gray eyes, just standing by, watching. Like so many were doing now.

I turned my eyes to Nash again, to the others. And then slowly, hesitantly, I nodded. I loosened my fingers from Nash's, started to pull my hand away.

"Wait!"

I stopped. Lander.

Mr. Dabir pressed the knife to his skin. Then Lander's brilliant blue eyes met mine, stared into them. He blinked and they softened. Then something else filled his deep pools of blue. Contentment.

"It's okay," he whispered the words, didn't look away.

My eyes widened and I shook my head.

Mr. Dabir let out a breath of frustration, a breath that had no patience left. He looked at me.

"Three."

"Lander!" I started to pull my fingers from Nash's again, to release my hand.

"Nash, don't let go of her hand," Lander said the words evenly, calmly.

Nash's eyes widened, but he clutched my fingers, held them tight. Alese held my other hand, frozen in place.

"Two."

Mr. Dabir clutched the knife with his fist. His eyes didn't move from mine.

"Lander, no!" I screamed the words, frantic. Distraught. "We can't do this without you."

We only knew what we felt, and that wasn't enough.

"Yes you can." Lander paused to take a breath. He clutched Mr. Dabir's hand that held the knife and light blond strands of hair fell over his forehead. "Just love. Love like it's the air you breathe."

"Enough!" Mr. Dabir's hands were shaking. His dark eyes narrowed and he grasped the knife more tightly. "Laney, he will die for nothing."

Lander looked at me once more. His blue eyes filled mine, and he smiled. "Don't ever forget that, do you hear me?"

"One."

"Don't ever forget that love is worth the fight."

Mr. Dabir paused for one more second. Then he slit Lander's throat.

44

"Lander, no!" I felt the words pass through my throat, and they echoed against the walls. Sucked the life out of the air.

I watched as Lander gasped for breath, clutched his throat with one hand.

Then Mr. Dabir let go.

Lander fell to the ground and his brilliant blue eyes looked out at the gray world again. One last time. Then his blond head hit the floor and his eyes closed, his body stilled.

I stumbled backward, watching in a daze. This wasn't real. It couldn't be real.

But Lander didn't move. He didn't breathe.

I collapsed on my knees, my hand still in Nash's. Mr. Dabir had killed him. And Lander had let him. Lander had died for this—for us.

He had died for love.

Mr. Dabir stood above the boy with blond hair, his knife still clutched in his fingers, waiting. Watching.

But we didn't let go. I wouldn't let go now, even if he killed each of us, one by one.

The room was silent. I heaved in shallow breaths, stared at the man who had killed the boy who had asked for nothing and yet had everything taken away. At the boy who had given Mr. Dabir another chance, even when he could have killed him. What kind of world was this?

I clenched my fists, and my eyes fell on the people who were still seated in the dismal chairs. The people who had watched him die.

Their heads were turned, farther than they had ever turned in thirteen years. Their tight buns faced me, their eyes staring down the aisle, past the chairs, at Mr. Dabir.

I grasped Nash's fingers more tightly. No, not Mr. Dabir. They were staring at Lander.

Carefully, slowly, the sea of gray turned forward again, looked at us. Didn't blink, didn't move.

Then, one by one, they began to press their hands to the edges of the chairs, plant their feet to the ground, and straighten their legs.

They began to stand.

I watched in silence. My heart was pounding in my head. The people didn't move. Didn't walk toward us or turn their heads again. They simply stood, feet rooted to the stone floor and pale faces looking forward. A moment passed. And then, in one single, soft movement, the person in the front and at the end of the row brought his hand up, toward the sky. I swallowed.

Like Nash had done. Like Nash had done with me.

Then the man brought his hand down and grasped the woman's hand next to him. As I watched, the person next to him did the same. And the next.

As each person grabbed the hand of the others, their eyes widened a little. The gray faded, and if you looked hard enough, you could see color hidden beneath the surface.

I watched in disbelief. Thought of the black box, the way the tiny figurines had twirled around the small platform. Maybe this is why people danced—for moments like this. My head felt dizzy.

But why? Why, after all these years—? I stopped. Lander's death. The way Lander died—chose to die—for us, that was love, wasn't it? The photograph showed love years ago, from the world above, between a man and a woman. Lander showed love down here, right now, between these gray walls. It was a different kind of love. But maybe that's the love they needed to see. For a brief, staggering moment I wondered if this was Lander's plan all along.

Arsen shifted from his place in the corner where he had been standing, frozen to the ground. Then he backed up a few steps, his eyes wide.

"Mr. Dabir, they're changing." He said the words in a single breath, horrified, and pointed to the chairs with a shaking finger.

I followed his gaze on the sea of gray. The people were looking at Lander again, with eyes filled with sadness and—compassion.

I blinked.

The gray in their eyes had faded to a thin mist, and the color—the blue, the green, and the brown—was beginning to shine through, like the sun.

Mr. Dabir watched, his mouth twisted in confusion. Arsen looked at him, then at us again. His eyes swept the room and landed on the door.

"I'm getting out of here." Arsen said the words frantically. He was panicking.

"Arsen, you will not leave." Mr. Dabir looked at him, and he tried to sound sure of himself, firm. But even Arsen saw through it.

Arsen looked at Mr. Dabir once more as he stepped down the aisle, crossed over to the door, and then stepped past him. Past Lander.

Then he started running, down the hall, toward the stairs. Up into the world.

Mr. Dabir watched him go, his knife frozen in the air. He blinked, and his chest moved in and out slowly. He looked down at the boy with blond hair, then back up, at all of us. He didn't move.

I clutched the fingers of the people beside me, spread my feet on the cool floor. Then I stood, slowly, carefully. I took in a deep, shaky breath. Lander's death—the boy who believed in love for a year even while he was in the depths of gray—couldn't be for nothing. It wouldn't be.

"Let's do something," I said the words, pushed the tears from my voice. Thought of the night by the water, under the black and white sky, and the day we were locked in the room in the Dome, both times when we "did something." But this time, we weren't having a competition. We wouldn't try to remember names or people or places. This time was different. This time, we would create these memories.

Nash looked at me, held my fingers tightly in his. Mr. Dabir's brows furrowed. His eyes narrowed slightly.

"Let's take a vote." I breathed in, turned to the others. Their eyes fell on me—the eyes of dozens of people who had lived thirteen years in a world of gray and most—or all—of their lives without love.

"All in favor of going up to the world above. Leaving this gray world behind forever."

There was a pause. Then the gray-haired man who had once had a family raised his hand. As he raised it, his hand was still clutched in the fingers of Gavin. He looked at him and Gavin nodded, raising his other hand. I watched as people scattered around the room raised their hands slowly, always bringing up the hand of the person next to them when they did. But that person never protested. None of them did.

Soon, the entire room was filled with hands clutching one another, raised up in choice—in victory. Hands raised like that first day, at Collaboration, when Nash had grasped my fingers and held my hand up for the world to see.

I took a deep, shaky breath. It was because of Lander. If they didn't believe in love before, they believed in it now. No one would die for something that didn't exist.

The room stilled. The sea of people watched me in silence. But this time, the silence was good.

I turned my eyes away and they fell on the man standing alone by the door. On the blond-haired boy lying beside him. Mr. Dabir thought he had killed love. I breathed in, clenched my fists. Love could never be killed. After all these years, it still existed in the trees, in the turquoise sky. It even existed in a world so deep underground that gray was all the people knew. I looked at the tall, bearded man. It was all he knew. I almost felt sorry for him.

"Mr. Dabir, we're leaving."

"But it wasn't unanimous!" Mr. Dabir sputtered the words, looked at us with wide eyes. "I didn't vote for it."

"Unanimous"—I looked back at him, didn't move my eyes from his—"isn't for the good of us all."

Mr. Dabir looked at me, looked at my eyes. Then he stumbled backward and his shoulders hit the wall. He turned, glanced around him, then at us again. His eyes fell on Lander once more before he backed away and hurried down the hall, into the world of gray.

I breathed in the thin air as I watched him leave. Felt my heartbeat slow. Stilled my shaking fingers. Then, slowly, I pulled them from the hands around me.

I walked into the circle and Theodore's green eyes filled mine. Relief rushed through me suddenly—he was going to be okay. I held out my hand, my brown eyes still wet, and he took it. I pulled him in a hug.

"Thank you," Theodore's body shook as he said the words. "Thank you."

I pulled away, nodded, smiled as best as I could.

Then Nash was next to me, and he pressed his hand under Theodore's arm, on his back, for support. Theodore looked at him in appreciation and tore his shirt, then wrapped the piece tightly around his leg.

Then he looked back at us, his green eyes shining.

"Let's go home."

The people of the Dome walked down the aisle and out the room's door as one, past the boy who had given his life. They each stopped next to him, stood for a moment by Lander. They didn't fully understand just what he had died for yet, but they would. And they knew that.

The footsteps echoed against the walls, but this time they didn't seem so dull. It was the first time we had walked together and had actually wanted to.

When we reached the hallway, I clutched Nash's arm. "Delma."

He looked at me, nodded, started to raise his hand to stop everyone.

"No." I looked around me, at the people. "Keep going. We'll catch up."

Nash looked into my eyes, and I thought of the smiling woman in the photograph. The man who held her hands without fear or doubt of what they had. Without fear or doubt of their love.

I smiled, held his hand for a moment longer. We may not have a house, or a place to go, but we had each other. We had the sky and the wind and the raindrops that fell from the sky. We had our friends. And that was enough. That was the greatest feeling I had ever felt.

I turned away from the people with eyes that were no longer as gray—no longer as glassed over as they once had been—and stepped down another hallway, into the dark classroom, then into another hallway, to the place we had been locked up.

As I passed Lander's room, I turned, looked through the door. I half-expected to see him there, his hands pressed against the glass, his blue eyes shining with laughter.

Delma stood the moment she saw me. Her wrinkled blue eyes widened.

I looked back, smiled softly. I held the card up to the door and it slid open.

She rushed over to me.

"It's okay. We're okay." My eyes fell, and I looked over at the room Lander had been in. Then I straightened, and my eyes met Delma's.

"The world above will be our home now. We'll be safe there."

Relief flashed through Delma's eyes.

I breathed in. "And thank you. Thank you for helping Theodore."

Delma took my hand in hers, patted it gently. "I knew you needed to be up there with them. I knew it all along."

Her lips formed into a smile and she walked past me, through the sliding door.

I stood there for a moment, thinking about what she had just said. Then I remembered something—how only six were supposed to go above ground, but Mr. Dabir had changed it to eight when someone nodded to him from the audience.

I spun around, looked at her as she turned the doorknob to the hallway. She looked back at me and winked.

Then her hands motioned me from the place where I stood in surprise, her words reached my ears.

"Everything is going to be okay now, Laney. Everything is going to be okay."

After that, we went to a place that no one in the Dome used to remember. Not until now.

We went up stairs for what seemed like seconds. When we finally reached the top floor, we walked into the small, gray room my friends and I had come into just days before. The door—the thick, gray door to the Dome—stood open, and my eyes filled with a burning, brilliant light. It didn't flicker, didn't dim. It stood there, unmoving, like it had a whole world to shine on.

The room was empty, and I could hear something in the world beyond the door. It wasn't fear, wasn't silence.

I sucked in my breath.

Someone was laughing. Laughter carried on the breeze, through the door, and into the gray room.

The people with gray eyes were already out there, in the world of color and light. Had already stepped through the door.

Delma took a deep breath and looked at me, a smile filling her cheeks. Her eyes.

Then she stepped through the wall of light and left me, standing alone in the silent room hundreds of feet above the Dome, listening to people who had managed to escape. People who were living out there now, in the world. People just like me.

I stepped forward, toward the light, felt the warmth of it on my face. Something pressed against my foot, and I stopped, looked down.

A yellow, wilting wildflower was lying just in front of the door.

Arsen. He must have dropped it there before he stepped through, into the world.

I knelt down, picked up the stem of the flower in my fingers. Looked at it for a moment.

Then I stood, clutching the wildflower in my hands before the world—the cold, gray world behind us and everything in it—would be destroyed.

45

I live in a world where love exists.

It is not a vision, a fragment of memory, because pieces of it live and breathe in our hearts and our minds.

This world isn't perfect. People like Arsen will always be out there, will always exist. Some may say that we're exactly where we started.

But to be able to hold a hand, to kiss, to cry bitter tears of joy, to help another stand—that will keep us going. That will be our reason to survive.

People may try to take it from us, try to strip this world of everything beautiful time and time again. But this time, we're waiting. This time, we're ready.

Why?

Because love is worth the fight.

Made in the USA
Lexington, KY
03 March 2017